Live for Something
Die for Nothing

By: Kevin Brown

Any references to historical events, real people, or real places are used fictitiously. Names, characters, and places are products of the authors imagination.

LIVE FOR SOMETHING DIE FOR NOTHING
Copyright © 2020 Kevin Brown

Printed in the United States of America

First Printing, 2020

For information contact:
Creators Cave LLC.
creatorscave@outlook.com

This book is dedicated to a special woman who supported me when I doubted myself and inspired me to be the best version of me. Though I cannot ever repay her. I will give it my best try.
&
To all those who take the time to read my book I am forever grateful and thank you for your support.

Enjoy!

Chapter I

Who Am I? (Pierce)

Life sure has a painful way of showing you that it is worth living. I am surprised to still be alive. A decision I made four years ago has led to life altering changes that are unimaginable. Now I find myself sitting on an uncomfortably stiff small chair in a room full of strangers. I looked around the room in agony repeatedly asking myself. "How did I end up here with all these screwed up people?" Yet somehow, I have always managed to find myself in the worst situations. Today is Christmas Eve and the highlight of my day will be attending a substance abuse group therapy session. However, as bad as it sounds. Things could be far worse.

While listening to another attendee who goes by Bob tell his story. I started to nod off while listening to him talk. I snapped out of its moments later when I heard Don's (group leader) deep voice. "Are we boring you?"

I awakened abruptly and noticed everyone in the group was staring at me. I felt like a complete ass. Using the back of my hand I quickly wiped the drool off of my mouth and cleared my throat. "No."

He smiled at me then picked up his notebook and pen. "Please introduce yourself to the group."

I crossed my arms and sat up in the chair. "Okay, my name is Pierce Kennedy Sr. I grew up in AC (Atlantic City, NJ). I'm 34 years old and I'm an ADDICT." It was odd calling myself an addict. Especially since I was not one.

Together everyone in the group welcomed me. "Hi Pierce."

Don tore a page out of his notebook and handed it to me. "Today is an important day for you, it's the first day of your recovery. We are all happy to share this moment with you. Do you want to share anything else with us?"

"No but what is this piece of paper for?"

"That's an assignment to help you with your recovery. I want you to fill in each one of the twelve numbered lines with the steps for N.A."

"And how is this going to help me with my situation?"

"You'll see. Give it a try. What do you have to lose? You can only go up from here." I responded with a blank expression. I did not want to admit it, but he was right.

Don went back to his seat and addressed the group. "In most cases things that we can feel, smell, hear, and see are the tools that are used to deceive us." He added, "We're most vulnerable when our focus is directed at the things that shine the brightest, speak the loudest, smell, or feel the best. However, we block out the fact that these things may not be good for us."

The picture that his words were painting became so vivid. I felt like he was talking to and about me. I thought about my life and the decisions I have made up until this point. It was one wrong decision after another, but the irony is at that time they felt so right. I thought that the only good decision was the one that led to my wallet being filled. It was not only about the money though. What made my choices even more alluring was the power and respect that came with it. That was even more invigorating then the money. It gave me a sense of validation as a man. It seemed like I was finally making something of myself and it felt good. Now the only thing left is pain and agony.

Every day I am haunted by the turmoil that has arisen from my past decisions. I cannot help but harp on the fact that it could have been avoided if I were not blinded by my own vanity. I had convinced myself that despite coming from nothing I had risen to the top of the world. That idea could not have been farther from the truth. It may have appeared that way on the outside but, I remained stagnant if not worse off than when I felt I had nothing. At the time I could not see it, but I already had exactly what I needed. I lost the two most important things to me. My wife and son. Now even in a room full of people I am all alone. I do not even have two pennies to rub together nor am I sure where to go from here.

Amidst the chatter my vision suddenly became blurry. I bent over in my chair and mumbled, "I can't see." I feel lightheaded and my anxiety starts to increase as the people around me are panicking. In the distance I hear the faint voice of Don going in and out.

"Pierce, Are you okay?" I feel like I am answering him but in reality, nothing is coming out of my mouth. I am terrified, nauseous, and confused. My breaths are rapid, and I cannot breathe. With the room spinning I try to stand up, but I cannot keep my balance. My clammy hands lose grip of the chair and I collapse on the floor and blackout.

I know you are wondering what my story is. Well, let me take you back to the beginning. My life started to change four years ago. I lived in the San Diego neighborhood East Village with my wife Riley and son Junior. We had an incredible high-rise condo with the most amazing view. Most nights for me would end standing on the balcony and looking out at the beautiful city skyline. I could also watch games going on at the ballpark from there. I personally was never much of a baseball fan, but that view made me grow an appreciation for the game. On top of that the weather was perfect and anything we needed was within walking distance. Despite all of the things in my life I felt I had nothing. I had not earned anything. Riley was the breadwinner. I was just lucky enough to be her husband.

Riley and Junior were the only family I had outside of my mother who I call by her first name Betty. To most people calling your mother by her first name would be disrespectful but they did not have a mother like mine. She is lucky I talk to her at all after what she has put me through. At that point I had not seen Betty in five years, but I felt bad, so I would give her a call every now and then to check up on her. She still lives in AC and after years of trying to help her. She struggled with drug addiction. Her drug of choice was pretty much anything she could get her hands on. It had been an ongoing battle for her since I was a boy. That is why she had not met her grandson. I decided not to expose my son to the disappointment and torment I had to endure as a child. It is a surprise she is still living but I guess it is like she always said, "It will take more than some ole drugs to take me out of my misery."

Growing up in AC times was hard with both my parents. My mom was a drug addict and my dad a drug dealer who was a drunk. They constantly argued and most of the time it would turn physical. During their altercations I would hide under my covers and cover my ears. When they were not fighting with each other he would tell me horrific stories about drug addicts, and she would tell me the same type of stories about alcoholics.

Now that I look back at it, they were not telling me those stories as lessons but instead to show me how much they despised each other. Despite the amount of time I spent around alcohol and drugs, I did not try my first drink or puff of weed until college. Even then I would only occasionally dabble in moderation. I refused to let drugs and alcohol take over my life like it did theirs. Between my mom using most of dad's drug supply, and him buying alcohol and gambling with the little money he did have. I did not have much growing up outside of the essentials. I can remember having to eat syrup sandwiches for breakfast, lunch, and dinner because it was the only thing in the apartment.

Things got worse when I turned five years old and my dad got sick. He had been complaining of chest pain for some time but refused to go to the doctors and get checked out. It was not until he had jaundice that he took it seriously. When he looked in the mirror and saw that his eyes had turned yellow it scared the crap out of him. He was diagnosed with an alcohol related liver disease. His years of drinking had finally caught up with him. He was only thirty-seven years old, but he had been drinking heavy since he was twelve. Even with his drinking problem I thought he was the best dad. He was all I had known up until that point. After the diagnoses he really tried to follow the doctor's orders to get better but none of his treatments were helping, and he needed a liver transplant. He even managed to stay sober for the six months needed to qualify for a liver.

From then on it was a waiting game. I was devastated by this news. I began to act out in school but managed to maintain good grades. Around this time Betty's drug problem started to get out of control. She walked out on us and was completely absent from my life from this time on. I can still hear the echo of her words saying, "I didn't sign up for this." I think it was a defense mechanism created from a mix of drugs and guilt. Unfortunately, I had to pay for it. I had to fill the void of taking care of dad and myself when she left. Dad ended up hanging in there and receiving a liver transplant three years later. His surgery is what inspired my dream of being a doctor. After the surgery we became really close. It is strange how you can get the good in someone when they are in a bad situation. The surgery gave him an extra four years before he passed due to complications in the summer of 1996. I am happy I at least got a chance to know who he was sober. I wished that were the only version of him I had ever known.

It was not all bad growing up though. There are some happy memories. The memories that stand out the most are with my best friend Zoe and her family. They moved to AC when I was twelve years old. We were going into middle school that upcoming fall. I had just lost my dad and was emotionally a wreck. I was hurt from losing him, but I still remember the first time I laid my eyes on her. In a way she made me forget about my pain and ultimately helped me heal.

I was this dusty kid wearing oversized clothes that previously belonged to my dad. She was the most strikingly beautiful girl I had ever seen. She had a pretty smile, dark brown eyes, and long full curly black hair. She was wearing a light blue floral ruffle day dress, floral print headband, and brown sandals. I would soon find out that her beauty was minor compared to who she was as a person. Her inner beauty glowed even brighter. She was empathetic, compassionate, and considerate. She became exactly who and what I needed at the time. To this day she has always been there for me through thick and thin and that means a lot considering all that I have been through.

Most of the things I learned in my teenage years came from the time I spent with her family. I have always loved them because they knew my situation but never judged me. Her dad Michael was a Navy man stationed in Philadelphia. He is dark skin, around six-foot-tall, stocky build, and has a buzz-cut with a clean shave. He always wore his shirts tucked in which I thought was funny but believe me he was not the type of guy you wanted to mess around with. He was a strict disciplinarian who did not take any crap. He scared me before I met him. However, I found out that you cannot judge a book by its cover. Once I got to know him, I saw that beneath the serious demeanor he was a genuine, funny, and caring guy. He was the first and only man that offered me any guidance. I saw him as a father figure and felt like he saw me as the son he never had.

Her mother Agatha was from Greece. They had met during his time stationed overseas in Crete. She is olive complexion, petite, light brown eyes, and has brunette hair that she usually wears in a ponytail. I immediately saw where her daughter got her beauty from. She was an ICU Nurse at Atlantic City Medical Center. Unfortunately, she had taken care of Betty as a patient on multiple occasions due to overdoses. Sadly, it happened so much it became the norm. It got to the point that when it happened, I expected her to recover from it like a common cold. I was not even embarrassed about it anymore. Agatha would always tell me that I knew and been through too much for a boy.

They did their best to bring some normalization to my life when I was around them. I spent holidays and birthdays with them. They allowed me to eat breakfast and dinner with them. There were weeks at a time I would stay at their house because I had not seen my mother for days. It was such a relief to not have to worry about where I was getting my next meal from. Agatha made the most delicious food. It was the only time I had homemade cooking. My favorite things she made were gyros and Greek almond cookies. I had finally felt like I had a family. It was something I always wanted. They embraced and supported me as if I were their own. Due to my instability at home who knows how things would have turned out for me without them.

Me and Zoe were pretty much inseparable until

college. I stayed in state and attended New Jersey State University. She went to an ivy league school in New York City. We would take the train to visit each other regularly early on for the first two years but as our coursework became more demanding, and we started to meet new people our availability began to shrink. On top of that I met Riley my junior year. She was not too fond of our relationship initially but despite that I had stayed in contact with Zoe and her parents through text, social media, and occasional calls. Zoe's now living in Margate and married to a great guy named Will who is a detective for AC. She is already a judge for the AC Municipal Court. However, her success does not surprise me at all. I had always known she would do great things and I could not be happier for her.

I also had a few friends in San Diego. They called me "caveman". If you saw me then you would know the nickname was earned on my part. I had a beard that was scruffy, a messy man bun, and wore the most basic outfits. My closest friends were Terry who is a Pain Management Doctor and Rich who works for US Mail Services. I have known Rich since my sophomore year in undergrad. He had transferred to the University that year from the community college. He was in ROTC and studying economics. I was majoring in pre-med. As you can imagine we both spent a lot of time in the campus library. We met there in a study group through mutual friends. He was one friend Riley did not mind me hanging around surprisingly since he was always getting into trouble.

We moved to California after undergrad because Riley was from San Francisco and wanted to go back out west to attend LA (Los Angeles) College of Law. I did not have any reason to stay home so I agreed to go. Shortly after we moved Rich decided to join us. He was fortunate to have parents with deep pockets. He took the year off to "figure" out what he wanted to do with his life. That year off consisted of partying, drinking, and drugs. Terry on the other hand is originally from LA. We met during my first and only semester at Southern California College of Medicine. We were both in the medicine program, but he actually finished.

After getting expelled I stayed in touch with him. I was on my way to becoming a doctor until I ran into some legal trouble. I wish Riley were a lawyer then because I sure could have used her help. I still wonder what I was thinking. I was so close to making my dream come true. I just knew being a doctor was my calling. For years I devoted all my time and energy to accomplishing that goal. That situation gave me a reality check. The cards for my life had already been dealt. My future would not be brighter than the darkness I had been running from.

It was always a matter of time before something would go wrong and derail my life. I have always withheld a bit of rage bottle up inside. It finally got the best of me and came out at the wrong time. This time it ended with me hurting someone during an altercation at a bar off campus. It happened during winter break while I was hanging out at a bar I had been to a few times before. However, this night a drunk guy stumbled into Riley and knocked her into another person causing her to spill her drink on herself. Afterwards, he just kept walking as if nothing happened. She was pissed and confronted him right away. He responded by getting in her face and calling her a "bitch" right in front me. I immediately got between them and we squared off. I could smell the vodka on his breath. The guy was clearly hammered but that was not an excuse. We exchanged words then he pushed me. I swung a punch hitting him in his face. Immediately after that I saw two of his friends coming toward me, so I grabbed a nearby chair and threw it at them.

Unfortunately, when I did that, I ended up badly injuring another person. The woman I hit was also with them. She ended up pressing charges on me. It was my first time getting into any trouble with the law. I was eventually charged with third degree assault and disturbing the peace. I got a hefty fine and three years' probation. I could not blame her though. She got caught in the crossfire of our situation and received multiple stitches for a gash right beneath her eye. I was expelled from school shortly after the incident. That night I became everything in life I despised. The events of that night played over and over in my mind for years. It took some time for me to cope with my actions and my reality as a result of it. Now I try to take life a day at a time. I tell myself, "It's progress not perfection."

Chapter II

Summer 14' (Pierce)

It was time for our family vacation of summer 2014. We had originally decided to go to Hawaii but out of nowhere Riley insisted we go to Hong Kong. Thank goodness we had insurance on our plane tickets so canceling our flights on such short notice did not cost us too much. We were visiting her parents. They had moved back to China from San Francisco a year prior. Riley felt it was time for Junior to experience and learn more about his heritage on her side of the family. He also had not seen his Grandfather Cheng and Grandmother Ju in a few months. They could not wait to see him. As for me this was not the ideal vacation by any stretch of the imagination.

Her family could be difficult to deal with at times. Her dad was always riding me, and her mom made it a point to make little sarcastic comments about me indirectly. I wanted to enjoy myself during the trip but each day I found myself thinking, "I'm one day closer to not having to see my in-laws for a while." After spending a week there, I was looking forward to a vacation away from them.

To begin my last morning there I started with a self-reflection exercise I got from my Psychiatrist, Dr. Amber Shaw. While gazing in the mirror I asked myself, "What do you see?" I stood there motionless looking deep into my own eyes. Various thoughts raced through my head uncontrollably. I reminded myself, "Don't think about it just say it." That had been the hardest question for me to answer throughout my life. The way I saw it was what is the point of asking that question when most likely what I saw was different from my reality.

Nonetheless Dr. Shaw insisted on me doing the exercise. She worried that my lack of introspection may cause me to lose myself even more. She would say jokingly, "At this point you couldn't see yourself in the mirror if you were in a mirror maze." The truth is she was right. I was consumed by everything I disliked about myself. My troubled past had caused me to suppress my feelings and lose sight of who I was.

During my therapy sessions I had learned life is about perspective. I needed to focus on the positives and not the negatives. However, that was easier said than done. Due to my anxiety I rarely had a clear mind. I was always worrying about what people thought of me. I formed opinions of myself through everyone else's eyes. To my lover I was once the perfect guy and now I am her biggest mistake. To her family I am a leech and dead weight. At work I am just another worker to call on to get the job done. To my friends I used to be the life of the party but now I am that guy who complains about what I could have been and how fucked up my life is. Ironically in public I tried to give off the impression to people that I had the perfect life.

I on the other hand considered myself to be a great prospect with so much untapped potential. I am handsome, smart, fun, and to top it off I am physically in great shape. I just needed to find a way to be happy with who I was and stop rationalizing for every aspect of my life I deemed as failure. I allowed my current status at that given time to define the totality of my life. At that point It would have been a win to be myself in public. I played so many different roles depending on who I was around or what environment I was in. I did not have the slightest clue of who I was anymore, but I knew it was time to take her advice seriously, and work on me.

As I continued to gaze in the mirror Riley began knocking on the bathroom door. I was trying to focus so I ignored her. She yelled, "Just meet us downstairs outside of the buffet for breakfast." In that moment I saw my life for what it really was. It was everything I thought my life would not be. As I looked deeper, I saw the same look I had seen as far back as I could remember. I appeared puzzled but certain I wanted the world for myself. I said repeatedly, "Today is my day, Today is my day, Today is my day." I felt something had to give. I understood that my dissatisfaction came from the fact that what I thought of myself did not align with my reality. My life was like a revolving door I could not exit. I felt like a prisoner to the life I was living. It was time to figure out what I wanted out of life. No more feeling sorry for myself.

After getting cleaned up I got dressed. I put on tan cargo shorts, an olive-green t-shirt, white tennis shoes, a sports watch, and sunglasses. When I got down to the lobby of the resort they were not there yet. I took a seat on the bench and began to daydream as I often do. I started dreaming about winning the lottery. I believed that if I won that money it would have made my life simpler. I could pay for my problems to go away. It would not solve everything, but it would have been a heck of a start. Suddenly, I heard the voices of my family conversing and the dream faded away. I joined them and greeted everyone. "Good morning. Everything okay?"

Riley smiled and turned to her mother. "We were in my parents room waiting for the diva to get dressed. Are you ready to eat?"

"Sure am," I replied with a disingenuous smile on my face.

It was my first time eating at the resort's buffet since we had been there. I had been staying up late every night so I could have some time alone. I had slept in most of our stay and by the time I would wake up breakfast would already be over. It turned out I had been missing out because the food they served was pretty good.

While we ate, I put on my usual performance which consisted of me laughing at her dad's jokes even though I was the butt of most of them. Then I pretended to care about the current gossip her mom talked about. Half of the time they talked in Mandarin knowing I could not understand. I went along with it despite knowing that they were probably talking shit about me behind my back but what could I do. They were her parents, my son's grandparents therefore I felt it was only right that I did. The only genuine moments of happiness I had during the trip was seeing the smile on my son's face. At least he was having a good time.

We spent our last day in Hong Kong at Causeway Bay. It was the part of the city where shoppers looking for luxury goods went. This trip would not have been complete for Riley without a shopping spree. We were staying in an upscale hotel in West Kowloon, so it was a short drive. When we arrived there the streets were busy, and the atmosphere was energetic. There were so many stores and people. We spent hours there going from place to place until Junior got hungry. Even then Riley did not want to stop. She always needed one more minute but eventually she gave in.

Cheng suggested we go to Food Street. When we got there the aroma of all the delicious food being cooked was enticing. I wanted food from every place selling it. While we were walking, we stumbled upon a Thai restaurant. Thai is one of my favorite types of food, so I asked everyone, "Who wants Thai?"

"Me," Junior shouted ecstatically. I turned my focus toward the rest of the group.

"Riley, Cheng, Ju?" They all looked at each other with uncertainty.

"Please," Junior pleaded. He had a way of getting what he wanted.

Everyone agreed and we got a table. We ordered Pad Thai and Thai Iced Tea. It was a great meal. We talked and laughed together as we enjoyed it. It is one of the better memories we have together as a family. I wanted to contribute to the trip so when we got the bill for our meal, I insisted that I paid. When the waitress came to collect the bill, I was searching for which pocket I put my wallet in. Meanwhile I could see that Riley was getting impatient. "Do you need me to pay," she asked in a displeased tone.

"Nope. I got it. I just need to find my wallet." I brushed it off and when I found my wallet, I gave the credit card to the waitress. After I signed the receipt, we continued to do more shopping since there were a few more stores that Riley wanted to go too. At this point my

16

stomach was full and standing around bored watching her shop was making me sleepy.

While we were watching her try on clothes Cheng received a phone call. He excused himself and stepped off to the side of the room. Based on his mannerisms he appeared to be in a serious conversation with someone. After hanging up the phone he called Riley and Ju over to discuss something. In the corner of my eye I saw them talking and watched as their smiles turned to more serious expressions. They walked back over to us and Riley said, "We have to go to an urgent business meeting for dad's company. You two can hang out still if you feel comfortable without us and we'll meet up with you later back at the hotel."

"Okay, we'll finish up here and catch a cab back to the hotel," I replied. She kissed us both goodbye and they flagged down a ride. At the time I was confused since she had not been involved in her father's business before but what did I know.

It was just me and Junior now. I figured since we spent all morning doing what Riley wanted to do. It was time to do something for him. Our first stop was the toy store. I let him get whatever he desired. I wanted his last day there to be fun and memorable. While I stood there watching him play with all the different toys, I was elated by his smile. He was so thrilled to be there. He explained all the features he liked about each toy to me. I can still hear his voice saying, "Daddy pick a toy so we can play together at home." At the time I brushed it off and let him choose a toy for us both. Now all I can think about is having the chance to play with him. To this day I have not experienced a better feeling than making him happy.

After leaving the store we explored the city some more. When we got back to the hotel the sun was still out, so we relaxed by the pool. I was exhausted but Junior was not and still wanted to play. That kid had no chill button. I asked him to give me ten minutes so I could rest for a moment. He liked to jump off the edge of the pool into my hands and get dipped under the water. Those joyful moments were the only thing that kept me sane. After about a half-hour we got out of the pool and dried off. He had to use the bathroom, so we went to the pool house. As he used the urinal, I waited for him at the sink. While looking at my reflection in the mirror. I remember thinking how I wanted every day to be like this, but I knew that was not going to happen if I did not make some changes. I had to find the inspiration somewhere. If not for me then for my son. I know what it is like to be let down by a parent. That was not an experience I was going to share with him.

Afterwards, we went back to our room to begin packing for our flight back home. We showered and took a nap. When we woke up it was seven o'clock and Riley still was not back yet. I called her phone but no answer, so I sent her a text message. Me and Junior could not wait any longer to eat so we went down to the buffet for dinner without her. We both got a stir-fry rice with shrimp. Shortly after we sat down to eat Riley walked over to us at the table. "I'll be right back down to join you two for dinner." When she walked away, I looked over at Junior and saw him playing with his food with his fork. "Eat your food Junior while it's hot. Mommy will be back in a few minutes. You don't have to wait for her to eat." In response he shrugged his shoulders.

After some time, Riley walked into the buffet and grabbed a plate. Junior spotted her in line and got up from his seat to join her. From a distance I could see him telling her what to get. When they came back to the table her plate had the same food we had gotten. "I see Junior sold you on the stir fry." We both laughed. It had been some time since I made her laugh. We continued to chat while we ate until we all finished with our meal.

We gathered our things and began walking back to the room when Junior suddenly stopped. He asked, "Are we eating dessert?" I looked at him with a grin.

"Would you like dessert?"

"Can I get some ice cream please?" I looked over at Riley.

"It's up to your mom." He turned his attention to her and gave her the googly eyes. She smiled and rubbed his head.

"Yes, you can. After all, what would vacation be without any desert."

I walked over to the food server and after he greeted me, I asked, "What kind of ice cream do you have?" He grabbed the ice cream scooper.

"We only have vanilla."

"I'll take a cup with rainbow sprinkles."

When I brought the cup over to Junior, he was delighted. On our way back to the room I watched as he ate the ice cream making a mess by getting it all over himself. I handed him a napkin to wipe his mouth off. Nonetheless he continued to eat sloppily. "Dad this is so good."

"Is it? Can I try some to make sure?"

"No. You'll eat it all." I laughed.

When we got back to our room Riley cleaned Junior

up and got him ready for bed. After he was tucked in, I asked Riley, "How did the business meeting go?" I could tell she did not want to talk about it because her response was a smirk and no response. She changed the subject.

"Are we all packed and set to leave tomorrow morning because I'm tired."

"Yes, me and Junior took care of that earlier." She was trying to avoid the question, but I did not let up on the issue. "I didn't know they had business meetings during national holiday's (Dragon Boat Festival) here." She started to get frustrated.

"Well things are done differently here. This is not the States. I'm going to take a shower before I go to sleep." She walked into the bathroom and locked the door behind her.

I stripped down to my boxers and laid in the bed. I laid there looking at the ceiling and thinking of all the changes I was going to make when I got back home. She came out of the bathroom ten minutes later and laid beside me gently. After a few minutes she rolled over and wrapped her arm around me. She pulled on my arm and tried to force me to reciprocate the action. I resisted her advancements, but she insisted. She whispered softly in my ear, "Can we make our last night here a good one?" As if I was the one with the problem. She then began to rub on my chest and kiss my neck. That was my weakness.

Next, she slowly directed my hand into her pants and reminded me why I may want to play nice. Of course, I fell for it and rolled over on my back. She got on top of me completely naked and began kissing me while pulling off my boxers. We then discretely went under the covers while Junior slept in the bed next to us. From that point on it was lights out. I was still pissed off at her, but I needed that moment. It provided an outlet for all my pent-up emotions. It was like once I climaxed all my issues dissolved temporarily.

The next morning, I woke up to Riley talking to Junior. When we made eye contact, she said, "I brought you up coffee and a cinnamon raisin bagel with butter. You should get up because the shuttle will be here in thirty minutes to take us to the airport."

"Cool," I replied barely awoke. I was still tired, so I laid there for a few more minutes with my eyes squinted looking at the ceiling. Once I got up, I went to the bathroom and got cleaned up. After I got out of the shower, I wiped the fog off the mirror with my hand and found myself staring at my reflection in the mirror again. Trying the exercise once more. I looked at myself and asked, "What do you see?" I embraced myself and replied, "All the potential in the world." I smiled at my reflection and then got dressed. As corny as it may sound that simple display of affection for myself felt good. I felt like there might be hope for me after all.

Chapter III

Back Home (Pierce)

I woke up to Junior shaking my arm and yelling. "Dad we're back!" When I opened my eyes and looked out the window the plane was taxiing to our gate. Dr. Shaw was right about the anti-anxiety pills she prescribed because they did wonders for me during the flight. Thankfully, I was able to sleep for most of it. After we exited the plane and headed over to the luggage area, I could see everything was back to normal. Riley was already on the phone fielding calls for work. Junior was playing with his handheld game console unaware of anything else going on around him.

After I got our bags off the belt and onto a cart, we headed to our car parked in the airport parking lot. "I'm hungry," said Junior. I suggested we grab lunch on the way home. Junior agreed but Riley said nothing as she was tapping on her cell phone screen.

"You guys grab lunch and I'll meet you home in a few hours. I have to meet with a client."

Even though I was not surprised about her response it still bothered me. "On a Saturday just getting back home from vacation. You have to work now?"

She sighed as she turned her face away from me. "I don't choose my hours. The business does and this is a major client." She kissed Junior and said, "See you later baby. Be good for daddy."

He looked down with disappointment on his face. "Okay mommy."

After we got into the car, I looked over my shoulder at Junior in the backseat. "What do you have a taste for buddy?"

His blank expression quickly turned into an excited grin. "Pizza!"

"Pizza it is."

I turned the music up and we drove to Tony's Pizza restaurant by our home. We ordered Juniors favorite. A large extra cheese pizza. While we were sitting down waiting for our food, I saw a friend of mine through the window. I told Junior, "Stay here and eat. I'll be right back." I ran outside and flagged him down. "Hey Mikey, what's going on?"

Initially he was startled by me catching him off guard. "What? Oh, hey what's up Pierce." We greeted each other then he said, "I did not know that was you. Anyway, you know me, I am trying to get some money. I just left the gym. Now I am headed to an in-home training session with a client in Torrey Pines. Did you just get back from your vacation? How was it?"

"Yea, we just got back not too long ago. Junior was hungry so we're getting some pizza, but it was a good trip. It's nice to get away sometimes you know."

He nodded his head in agreeance while he looked down at his watch. "Yea, I need a vacation myself, but I got to run. Let us finish this conversation during our next workout. Text me your availability and we will set something up. Talk to you later."

"Will do. Later." We shook hands before we went our separate ways.

Mikey had been my trainer for the past three years. I meant him while I was walking out of that same pizza restaurant. He convinced me to do boxing training and it turned out to be a good thing for me. The workouts gave me an outlet to release my stress. Plus, it was nice to go away from doing my usual weightlifting and running workout routine.

On the way back inside the restaurant a man stopped me at the door. He had a haunted look on his face and no teeth. He slowly extended his hand out to me. "Do you have any spare cash sir?" I reached into my pocket and gave him the change from my pizza. It was five dollars and sixty cents. "Thanks man you're a lifesaver." As he walked away, I asked myself, "Is there any difference between me and that man?" Based on how my life had been up until that point I could not think of any.

I am sure neither one of us was living the life of our dreams. I stood in the doorway momentarily lost in thought. "Dad the pizza is getting cold!" I snapped out of it and headed back to my table rubbing my hands together in anticipation of a tasty slice of pizza. I grabbed the garlic salt, red pepper flakes, and parmesan cheese. "Let's dig in." Junior watched as I sprinkled seasoning on my slice.

"Can you put parmesan cheese on my half?"

"You got it buddy. I am going to make sure you get anything you want. You understand?" He looked somewhat confused, but I knew in time he would understand what I was saying.

"Yes. Thanks daddy."

Before biting into my slice, I thought to myself, "I'm nothing like the man I had just encountered because I'm going to make something of myself."

After eating we were finally home. It was six o'clock and still no Riley. It was a pattern with her. She spent more time away from home then with us. To cap off the night me and Junior watched a movie together. Then we went to brush our teeth before I put him to bed. When I laid down, I sent her a text that got no reply. An hour or so later I heard the door shut. I waited anxiously in bed until she got to the room. First, she stopped by Junior's room. "Goodnight," she said in a soft tone. Then she closed the door and began walking toward the room. I could hear the clicking of her heels on the floor as she approached.

She walked in and looked at me with an awkward expression on her face. "Sorry the meeting ran later then I thought it would."

I was furious but kept my composure. "I left some pizza downstairs for you in the microwave."

"Thanks, but I'm not hungry. I took my client out to eat."

She went into the bathroom, shut the door, and turned on the shower. I felt like something was up with her. I knew we were not on the best of terms in our relationship but there was something else going on. I wanted to go to sleep so I did not have to deal with the situation, but I could not. Several ideas of what she was up to continuously ran through my mind. My throat felt dry, heart was racing, and eyes began twitching from frustration. I walked down to the kitchen and got me a glass of water. I was trying everything I could think of to relax myself.

When she came out of the bathroom, I was sitting on the side of the bed with my back turned to her. I acted like she was not there to avoid any confrontation. She sat down and turned on her nightstand light. She started looking over some papers and the sound of them shuffling irritated me even more. I laid down on my side and stared at the clock on my nightstand. It felt like time was standing still and I could not take the torment. I eventually started to fall asleep until I heard her phone vibrate followed by a giggle. That was the final straw. I turned around and confronted her.

"Riley what's going on with you, what is it, who is it that causes you to spend so much time away from us?"

She slammed her phone down on the nightstand. "Pierce it's no concern of yours."

I hinted at stuff before, but this was the first time I pushed the issue and was persistent. "That's not an answer and I need you to give me one." She began shaking her head side to side while continuing to look at her papers with an aggravated expression on her face. "Hello, I'm waiting."

"If you're accusing me of cheating, be a man and say it. Like I said many times before it is business. Somebody has to pay for all this shit we have," she replied with disdain in her voice. Then she grabbed her bag, papers, phone, and got out of the bed. "I'll sleep in the guest room tonight!"

There was no way I was going to be able to sleep now. I needed to get out of the house and blow off some steam. I got out of the bed, put on some clothes, and left the condo. I walked a couple blocks from my home to a local bar called McSwiggan's. Before I walked in, I stood outside for a moment to think. I spent that time going over in my mind about what just happened. I could not come to a solution that would satisfy me, so I decided to forget about it. I thought to myself, "Fuck it. I'm getting a beer."

I sat at the bar alone sipping on my beer waiting for the buzz to kick in. I thought about calling Terry and Rich to join me but that would have only made it worse. I would have to explain what was going on to them and I would rather not. I did not want any advice or to be judged. I needed to calm down and relax my mind. It was best to forget everything and reset. If I was ever going to turn the page in my life there was no time better, then now. I got a shot and let my mind go free while talking and flirting with the hot bartender.

Suddenly, I heard some commotion in the back of the bar. In the crowd of people, I saw two women carrying their friend outside. Her head was slumped down, spit was hanging from her lip, eyes were closed, and feet were dragging on the ground with each step. I never understood why people got that drunk. I felt like it defeated the purpose. When they were exiting the building, I heard a man foolishly shout, "Somebody had a goodnight." I did not see it that way. It reminded me of the times when I walked in my home as a child and would see my dad unresponsive on the floor with puke next to him. Those were some of the most dreadful moments in my life.

It was getting late, so I paid my bill. As I was getting ready to leave. I felt a tap on the shoulder. I turned around and it was a beautiful woman in a tight red dress. She was so fine, and I was not the only person who knew it. I could feel the eyes of all the other guys in the bar staring at us. She said something to me, but I could not hear her over the music blaring in the background. I figured she just wanted my seat, so I told her that I was leaving. She pulled me closer and placed her hands up to my ear. "Why so early? The night is still young!"

Not sure if I heard her correctly, I said the first thing that came to my mind. "It's past my bedtime." However, she was not buying it.

"Have a drink with me?"

I usually would avoid situations like that but that night I wanted to try something different. Plus, she was stunning, so I felt obligated to accompany her. "Okay I can stay for a drink."

"Great. It will be fun. You will see. What are you drinking?"

"I'll take a beer."

"C'mon, I'm treating, and you want a boring beer?"

"Okay, I'll have what you're drinking but only one drink."

"You're kidding me. Can we at least agree to see how the first one goes before you call it quits?"

I hesitated before responding but she drove a hard bargain. "Sure, why not and I'll do you one better. I'll pay."

"Lucky me," as she smiled then she ordered us two gin and tonics.

While we were waiting for our drinks, she extended her hand out to me. "I'm Natalie by the way."

I reciprocate the gesture. "Nice to meet you. I'm Pierce."

The bartender gave us our drinks and I gave her my card. She asked, "Do you want to start a tab?"

"No. I'll pay now." I gave Natalie her drink and watched as she sipped from the straw.

She smiled when she caught me looking at her. She put her drink down on the counter and placed her hand on my shoulder. "Who are you here with?"

"I'm alone." She laughed and laughed with her even though I was unsure of what was so funny. "Is there something wrong with that?"

"Nope. It's perfectly normal I hang out at the bar by myself all the time," she sarcastically replied.

"I just wanted to get out of the house for a while." "I wasn't making fun of you. I promise. It is just I saw you have a ring on, and you are a good-looking guy. If you were mine, I wouldn't let you go out alone."

For a moment I found myself drawn in by her words and captivated by beautiful green eyes. Before things got out of control, I quickly changed the subject. "Are you here alone?" She pointed over to a group of women dancing on the floor. They looked back at us and started celebrating the fact that we were talking. "I didn't know we had an audience."

The bartender gave me the receipt to sign. I reached into my pocket and put some cash on the bar for the tip. Natalie asked, "Do you live here in East Village?"

"Yea I do. How about you?"

"I stay in Carmel Valley."

"Fancy," we both laughed.

"I try. What do you do for a living?"

"I'm a truck driver for now. You?"

"I'm in entertainment. Why do you say that for now? Is there something else you'd rather be doing?"

"Yea I would like to do something else. My job now was not my first choice. I just don't know what I want to do yet."

"You'll figure it out. There is no rush. You're still

young."

"How old do you think I am?"

"I would guess that you're around thirty-five?"

My face cringed. "Geez I look that old?" We laughed. "I'm twenty-eight."

"In that case you may be too young for me" We laughed. "How old do you think I am?"

"Twenty-seven."

"Nope twenty-three. No one ever guesses the right age. I guess it's because I'm so mature," she said jokingly.

"Well either way you look amazing."

"Thank you," as she blushed.

We finished our drinks and she said, "Dance with me." She grabbed my hand and led me to the dance floor. We went hard for about five songs straight. We were all over each other like we have been searching for each other our whole lives. When she grinded on me I experienced lust like I never had before. As my hands glided across her soft and smooth skin, she became all I ever dreamed of. Her touch and scent gave me a euphoric experience that I never had before. I reveled in the moment and wanted it to last forever.

As the last song was going off, she stopped dancing and looked at me. "Do you want to get out of here?"

At first, I was skeptical and still teetering the fence about whether or not what I was doing was okay. "And go where?"

"We could go grab something to eat from a place nearby."

"What about your friends?"

"They'll be okay. I already texted them that we were leaving?"

"Is this something you do all the time?"

"Never but it's something about you. Are you in?"

The situation seemed too good to be true. For all I knew she could be luring me somewhere as a setup. Regardless it was a risk that I was willing to take. "Sure."

We ended up going to a ramen noodle restaurant. I recommended that we sit at the bar to keep this outing casual and she respected it. While I was looking at the menu she asked, "What are you going to get?"

"Not sure. This is my first-time eating Ramen."

"Well, what do you have a taste for?"

I wanted to say, "You." But instead I replied, "Whatever you get. Surprise me."

"We can get Chicken Ramen. How's that sound?"

"That works for me." She placed two orders of chicken ramen and added two sake bombs.

Caught off guard by the drinks I questioned her. "Who are the drinks for?"

"For us."

"I've already exceeded my limit for the night."

"You need to loosen up and enjoy yourself. Are you always this uptight?"

Even though I was reluctant to hear it she had a point. I did need to relax and enjoy myself. After all that is why I came out tonight. "Okay, bring it on."

Next thing I know we had eaten our Ramen and were three sake bombs deep. When we left the restaurant, I could barely walk straight. It was two o'clock in the morning and I wondered how Riley was feeling now that I was the one out late.

I told Natalie, "Thanks for tonight. You have no idea how much I needed this. Thank you."

31

She smiled and gave me a kiss on the cheek. "I've had a great time with you too, but the night doesn't have to end here?"

Between the alcohol and her admiration for me. My ego was at an all-time high. "What else do you have in mind?"

"For starters I could use a ride home since I rode here with my friends and they're gone."

"Since we've both been drinking. How about I get us a ride on the car service app."

"That's perfect."

I was tipsy but I knew I had to be cautious. I could not be seen riding around with her in my truck. I got her address and placed it in the app. The car arrived nine minutes later and just like that we were headed to her house. I could not believe I was entertaining this. I was so nervous that I sat in the front passenger seat while she was in the back. While we were riding, she rubbed her finger across my neck. "You didn't have to sit in the front. I won't bite you."

I thought to myself, "You might not but I will."

She stayed on a corner lot in a big Mediterranean style home. The property was beautiful. It had a well-manicured lawn, garden, and a pool in the backyard that overlooked the ocean. When we got out of the car the first thing I said was, "Nice house. Do you live here alone?"

"You can say that. I'm always here alone." She opened the front door and said, "Make yourself at home. Would you like red or white wine?"

"I'll take red."

She poured us both a glass of red wine and sat next to me. She placed her hand on my thigh and looked me in my eyes. "What do you want to get out of tonight?"

"Just your company is good enough," I replied timidly.

She looked down at my pants and saw my manhood imprint. "It looks like your friend has something else in mind."

I could not contain myself. I wanted her so bad. She kissed me and I tensed up. When she stopped, I placed my glass on the table and grabbed her hands. "I can't do this."

"Did I do something wrong?"

"No, you're a breath of fresh air and under different circumstances I'd be all over you. But now is not the time. Even though my marriage is shit. I'm still married."

"I'm sorry. You are right. I wish the guys I dated had the same morals."

"I should get out of here." I ordered a ride on the car service app back to my truck. Before leaving I gave her a hug. "I really did have a good time with you."

She smiled and walked me over to the front door. "Maybe we'll meet again on different terms."

"Maybe."

I still had twelve minutes before my car came so I went out front and sat on the curb. I did not know if that night was a step in the right direction, but it sure did feel good.

Chapter IV

Big Business (Riley)

Now that we are back home Pierce is back to his insecure ways. He is always starting arguments with me over every little thing. Either it's I work too much, I work too late, or I do not support him enough. He tends to over analyze everything I do and not focus on what it is he should be doing. What does he expect from me? I feel like I am handling everything in both our lives alone. Over the past few years, he has been in a depressed state of mind and it has started to trickle down to me. If he had to handle half of what I was dealing with he would have fallen apart.

Apparently, I am selfish, but he is continuously sucking the life out of me with his issues. I love him but, in this case, misery will not be having company. When I look back on our relationship, I do not know how we got to this point but were here. I no longer hope for him to change. I understand who he is now. We are bonded through our son and that is what keeps us together. At this point I cannot worry about what Pierce has going on. It is going to take every bit of my energy to take care of our son, continue growing my firm, and help my father with his business. Though Pierce is annoying at least he is still a treat to look at.

While I lay in the quiet guest room with a glimmer

of light coming from outside the window. I thought about what had transpired over vacation. Prior to the trip it had been some time since I last saw my parents. It was nice to spend time with them and having Junior there made it that much better. The trip was ideal until I was blindsided by my dad asking me to be involved in his business. I should have sensed that there was more to the trip when he insisted on me coming to visit. I still do not understand what drove him to the decision of involving me in the same business he always kept me away from. I am sure my drug addict for a brother Ray's inability to be trusted had an influence. Therefore, the responsibility now falls on me.

After all this time in San Diego I forgot how congested Hong Kong was. I have grown to appreciate the less hectic city life. However, I did get a chance to enjoy myself while being there. I was able to do my two favorite things which are to spend time with my baby and shop. The energy of the people was so vibrant. It was a nice change of scenery for me. Nevertheless, the last day there changed the dynamic of the trip.

I woke up that morning to Junior watching a cartoon. I said to him, "How did you sleep baby?"

"Good."

"No more tv. Go brush your teeth and wash your face so we can go to breakfast."

I looked over at Pierce as he laid in bed snoring. I do not know how he can sleep with the TV so loud. I walked over to Pierce and nudged his arm. "Get up we're going to breakfast soon."

He moved his arm and mumbled. "Five more minutes."

"You better get up. We're going to have breakfast

together at least one time on this trip and today is our last day."

While he got himself together, I helped Junior get dressed. However, I wore a designer flare dress, sandals, tote bag, and sunglasses. We were ready to head out and as usual Pierce was in the bathroom taking his time. I knocked on the door and got no response. I received a text from my dad that read, "Meet me in my room." I continued to knock on the door to no avail. "Just meet us downstairs outside of the buffet for breakfast!" He did not respond but I knew he heard me.

I had the key card for my parents' room so me and Junior just walked in. My parents greeted us and then my dad said, "Let's talk on the patio."

My mom grabbed Junior's hand, "Lets watch TV while they talk."

He shut the balcony door behind us. "Today there is a meeting set up with us and a potential partner in regard to expanding the business."

I was confused and had no idea why he was telling me this. "What does that have to do with me?"

He leaned forward and looked me in my eyes. "I'd like you to join me."

Still lost and unsure of what was going on. I clenched my hands together and sat them on my lap. "Is this why you had me come here?"

He put his hand on top of mines. "No, I asked you to come here to see my daughter and grandson, but this is a great opportunity for us to grow the family business."

"And what exactly is the family business?" The truth is I never really knew what my father did for a living. However, I always got what I needed and wanted to grow up. Up until now I had never questioned it.

"Drugs."

I stood up out of my seat. "Wait. Are you asking me to deal street drugs with you?"

"Relax and sit down. I'm talking about making drugs for a pharmaceutical company."

I sat back down. "So, what are you asking of me?"

"The deal I have with my potential partner is conditional."

"What does that mean?"

"It means I promised I'd get us a U.S. customer and approved for a license by the FDA. That is where you come in. I need you to get us quickly approved by the FDA and convince one of your pharmaceutical clients to take us on as their supplier."

I was speechless. I did not see this coming at all. Nonetheless, I had to say something. "Dad. It is not that simple. I cannot just reach out to people and ask them to go into business with anybody who makes drugs. They wouldn't take the risk, nor would I advise them too."

"We're not just anybody. My partners are a legit API manufacturer. They already have customers in London, Paris, and Switzerland. This is our opportunity to help them get into the US and make a lot of money. If this deal went through, I could finally retire and know my family will be set long after I'm gone." He continued on to say, "I know I've kept you away from the business so you can have a chance to live your own life. I still want the same thing for you. I just need your help with this one little thing." I looked down with a blank expression knowing I could not defy my father. He put his hand under my chin and lifted my head. "Can I count on you?"

I was reluctant to reply but I felt like I only had one option. It was inevitable that this was going to be a part of my life. I hesitated for a moment as I looked at him. "Always dad."

My father had always been successful at everything he had pursued. I trusted that he would not ask me to assist him with something that would put me in harm's way.

Later that day we met his potential partners at an office building in Central Hong Kong. He filled me in on the details of the deal on the way there. The drug was an opioid painkiller. Essentially, after we got the license approval and a customer, he would make twenty five percent of the drugs and profit from the deal. My role was to establish the relationship between both sides.

When we arrived at the building and walked into the room there were three men wearing suits inside. They greeted us as we joined them at the oval table. The men expressed to my father how grateful they were for him taking the time to meet with them. They proceeded to tell him what they hoped to get out of the partnership and how profitable this opportunity could be for them both. Before they began discussing the particulars of their business my father introduced me and made it clear that I would be handling the business expansion to the U.S. I was not sure how they perceived me since they did not make eye contact with me once from the time, I entered the room.

The first question posed to me was by the man who sat at the head of the table. "What makes you qualified to take on this task?"

I knew that my involvement would bring about doubt. Nonetheless, their assumptions about me could not have been farther from the truth. My father explained to them I was the one person who could make their dreams a reality. Truth be told their doubt fueled me even more to make the deal happen and prove them wrong. I turned my attention to him and addressed his concerns. "It's clear you all have your doubts but let me assure you that whatever it is you think of me it doesn't change the fact that I'm your best and only option. I already have established relationships with multiple companies in the U.S. The same companies we all plan to do business with, and I guarantee to make it happen. Nothing more. Nothing less."

He looked fiercely at me for a moment before smiling. "Okay. We're in." It was followed by agreement from the others. He continued on to say, "The deal is seventy five percent of the business goes to us and we let you have twenty five percent. Deal?"

Before my father could say anything, I chimed in. "No. 50/50 split, or we walk and take this deal to someone else."

He looked over at my dad in confusion. "She's making the deal for you now?"

"You heard what she said. 50/50."

In the corner of my eye I could see my father grinning. The man looked at the other men sitting at the table. I watched as they all nodded their heads. He sighed then turned his attention back to me. "When do we start?"

My dad interceded and replied, "We'll be in touch after we get everything set up on our end."

As the thought of the trip faded away, I heard a knock at the door. I got up, unlocked it, and aggressively opened the door. To my surprise it was Junior. I said,

"What's wrong baby?"

"I can't sleep."

I invited him inside the room. "I can't sleep either. You can sleep with me."

As we laid there, I ran my fingers through his hair. That always helped him relax and fall asleep. In a way when he was relaxed it allowed me to be as well. Before I went to sleep, I thought of the challenge ahead. This would take my dad's business to heights it has never been. The burden of executing this in such a small-time frame while still dealing with my own life was stressful but I knew there was not any time for worrying. On top of that there was no way out. I had to get it done by any means necessary.

Chapter V

Back to the Bull (Pierce)

The next morning, I woke up to the annoying sound of my alarm clock. I did not remember when I got home the night before, but I knew I had a great time. However, I was still pissed off about my argument with Riley. I had a hangover and it was a struggle getting out of the bed. I was thirsty and had a throbbing headache. Before standing up I took a moment and sat on the side of the bed with my head slumped down facing the floor. When I finally got up, I walked to the guest room to speak with Riley.

I opened the bedroom door and found Junior sleeping. Riley had already gone to work. I woke him up and we got ready for the day. I made us a quick breakfast aka cereal. After we ate, I packed Juniors lunch and we got inside the other love of my life. My supercharged pickup truck. It had matte black paint job, tinted windows, black custom wheels, and over 600 hp. I called it the Black Beast. It was a thing of beauty.

On the way to his school I noticed he seemed bothered. He was withdrawn and staring out the window. I turned down the radio and asked him, "Is everything okay buddy?"

"Mhm," he replied while continuing to stare out the window.

"How is school?"

"Fine."

All he was giving me was one-word answers so I could tell something was bothering him. I felt helpless when I could not fix his problems. The rest of the ride was quiet. I figured it was best to give him space and when he was ready to talk, he would.

When we arrived at the school, he just got out of the truck without saying anything. I rolled down the passenger side window. "Have a good day. I will see you after school. Love you." He responded with an unenthusiastic wave. I sat there and watched him walk into the building. I figured whatever was bothering him would soon pass.

I needed something to boost my energy, so I stopped for coffee at a cafe two blocks away. I got my daily Frappuccino, took a sip, and "Ah," refreshing. Once I got back into the truck, I called Riley on her cell phone. It rang for a while then went to her voicemail. Midway through me leaving her a voicemail she was calling me back.

I answered and said, "Hello."

"Yes."

"Riley I…" Before I could finish what, I was saying she cut me off mid sentence.

"No need to say anything Pierce you're right I need to focus more on our family."

I was dumbfounded by her statement and responded with silence. Yes, this is what I wanted to hear but never expected it to be that easy. I asked myself. Why now? What is her agenda? She then insisted that we go out for dinner. I wanted to see how things would play out, so I went along with it. "Okay."

"Is there anywhere specific you would like to go?"

"Actually, there is a place called Nina's Kitchen. I heard it has great food and music."

"That's where we'll go then. It is a date. And Pierce it will be different from now on. Better. Just meet me halfway. I'll text you later with the time."

"Alright I'll talk to you later."

When I looked back at our relationship it was clear that she did not respect me at all. She talks a good game, but her actions have continuously shown me otherwise. I guess it is true what people say. You become attracted to what you're used to whether it is good or bad for you. She was nothing like my mother but at times the way she made me feel was the same. Insignificant.

I pulled into the staff parking lot at work and parked in the back away from the other cars. I looked in my rear-view mirror and performed my self-reflection exercises before getting out of the truck. On the way into the warehouse I saw James (coworker) and Mike (Warehouse Manager). They were talking while smoking their morning cigarettes. I never understood why they had to do it in front of the entrance. I hate the smell of cigarettes. Other than that, they were okay guys.

James was funny but he talked too much. He would always ask a bunch of random questions. It felt like he was interrogating you. Mike on the other hand was a hard ass and by the book. I could tell he got off on flexing his power, but he was easy to work for if you did your job. As I approached them James said, "What's up bro! How was your trip?"

"It was a good escape from here. Now I'm back." We all laughed.

Mike added, "Well if it's any consolation we missed

you. Also, we're behind on pick-ups and I need you on the Tijuana route today. The paperwork is in the office."

"Alright, see you guys inside."

Once inside the building I went into the locker room. I opened my locker and changed into my work outfit. I looked inside my locker door and saw the picture of me and Junior when he had just turned one. It reminded me why I had to stay positive and work through whatever it was I had going on. I walked into the office to get the paperwork and the keys to the truck I was assigned to drive.

Mike walked in the office as I was leaving and stopped me. "It's a big load and time is of the essence. There has been a shortage of product in the area. I'm counting on you." I responded with a faint smile. He took the importance of our job way too seriously. After all it's only candy that we are delivering. I did a quick inspection of the truck, got inside of it, and plugged in my aux cord. Once I got my music set up, I was ready to ride. The facility in Tijuana was only twenty miles away but it is about an hour ride with the traffic.

As I was closing in on the border crossing, I got into the fast lane even though I did not think it made the wait any shorter. While approaching the booth I received a text from Riley. It read, "Let's do tonight at 8." I quickly replied, "Sounds good." She responded back with a smiley face. When the border patrol agent got to me, he asked for my documentation and I handed it over. He looked over it briefly and said, "You're all set. Enjoy your time in Mexico."

I took my documentation back and replied, "Gracias." It was one of the few words I knew in Spanish, so I jumped on any opportunity to use it.

When I got to the warehouse lot Jose (dock worker) directed me to the open loading door. He yelled, "Spot four." I backed into the spot and when I got out of the truck, he ran up to me. "Where have you been vato? I thought you quit." We laughed.

"I wish. I was on vacation but I'm back now. What's new?" He had been at the warehouse for about six months and every time we saw each other we would bust each other's balls. He suddenly stopped smiling and looked at me.

"Now that you ask there is something new. I got a proposition for you?"

"What is it?"

"Not here though. Walk with me over to the break area." I did not think much of it because he was always playing around. I figured he just wanted company while he smoked. When we got to the break area, he offered me a cigarette.

"No thanks." He lit his cigarette and scoped out the surroundings as if he had something to hide.

In a low discrete voice, he said, "How do you like your job?"

"It's a job."

"Well, I have an idea to make it better for you."

"I'm listening."

"There is going to be additional merchandise with your load."

"Additional," I replied inquisitively.

"Yea, you won't even notice it. Just drive your load back to your facility in San Diego like you normally do. We have people over there to take care of the rest. There's a thousand dollars in it for you." I was unsure of what he was asking of me and started to feel apprehensive.

"I don't know Jose. What is it and how much of it will I be carrying?" I was not naïve though. I had a good idea of what it was.

"You don't have to worry about it. Trust me. This is basically free money, but I need an answer now. This is your chance."

He stared at me fiercely with his eyebrows slightly raised waiting for me to say yes. I paused for a moment and thought to myself, "He must be crazy. My life is fucked up enough. The last thing I need is to be getting caught up in some shit. However, it sounds low risk and could be easy money. Maybe this is my opportunity. A chance to do something for me. Make something of myself. I would be able to get my wife and son something nice for a change with my own money. This could be something I do for myself. Nobody will know. I can do it. I can do it." I looked up at Jose and replied, "I can do it."

"Muy Bien. You are now a part of our family and there is no turning back. If there is any sign that you are fucking us in any way it will not end well for you or me. I can count on you right?"

"Sure." We shook hands and started walking back toward my truck. He made a gesture to a man on the dock then turned to me.

"Everything is all set. Just be normal. Nothing is different. Do not be suspicious and do what you have been doing. If everything goes well. I'll see you on your next trip mi amigo."

"Who will I be giving the load to when I get there?"

"After you park the truck at Dash our people will take care of it from there. Like I said before just do what you always do. This is just another day at work."

"Alright, I'm good. I'll see you later."

When they finished loading the truck, I nervously went into the office to get the paperwork for my return. I could not believe what I was about to do. I needed to relax so I told myself, "This isn't a big deal. I got this." The office employee asked, "Is everything listed on the paperwork in the truck." I hesitated for a moment because I felt like I had already gotten busted and I did not even leave the dock yet.

"Um. Yes."

"I just need you to confirm it." She handed me the paperwork and said, "Sign by the X."

After I signed, she handed me my copy. I took the documents and walked slowly to the truck. It was the longest walk in my life. I got into the truck and did not want to leave the dock. I sat there in a moment of uncertainty. I knew I could not change my mind though. I was trying to work up some courage to get on the road. After a few minutes I pulled off. When I approached the border, I tried to remain composed on the outside but inside I wanted to yell. The officer came to the window and asked for my documents. The other officers did their search of my truck which felt like forever, but everything checked out. When the officer used the words, "Your good to go. Safe travels."

I wanted to celebrate but instead I replied, "Thank you."

However, he had no idea of how thankful I was. Once I was in the clear. I felt the monkey jump off my back. It was such a relief. It felt like I was being given my life back. My shirt was soaked from anxiety and paranoia. It may have blown my cover if it was not so hot that day. When I was back in California I basked in a moment of invincibility. It was refreshing to feel like I was in control again. The rest of the ride was a breeze.

When I got back to Dash I did exactly what Jose instructed me to do. I parked the truck and left it there to be unloaded. I walked into the office and Mike said, "Great timing. I knew I could count on you. How was the trip?"

"Just another trip."

"Well I'm happy your back. Now you can make a few local runs in the van."

"Lucky me."

After I left the office. I went to the bathroom. I checked the stalls to make sure nobody else was in there. After I saw the coast was clear I looked in the mirror and started laughing hysterically. I exclaimed, "Today is my day, Today is my day, Today is my fucking day!" It was such a rush. I finally took some initiative and I liked the feeling. It didn't dawn on me that the feeling of wholeness I was experiencing would start a domino effect of misguided actions for years to follow.

After making my runs I went back into the facility and went to my locker. I changed out of my work outfit but still had ten minutes until five o'clock, so I sat on the bench by the time clock. I scrolled through my phone looking at my social media account timeline until it was time to clock out. While walking to the car Riley sent me a text that read, "I picked up Junior from the afterschool program so you can come straight home to get ready for tonight." I had forgotten all about going out, but I was excited about it. I finally had something to celebrate even though I could not share the news with anyone else.

When I got home, Riley had already called Emily, our babysitter. She was a neighborhood teenager who was saving up money for a car. Junior loved when she came over. He always talked about how much fun he had with her. Also, apparently, he felt like she was the only person who understood him. I think he had a crush on her but he was at that age where he still thought that was nasty so he would not admit it.

I greeted Emily when I walked through the door, hugged Junior, and kissed Riley. I complimented Riley on her blue evening gown she had on. She looked stunning. She re-insured me that we were going to have fun that night as she smacked my butt. I ran upstairs and got cleaned up. I figured I would try a different look. I started by shaving my beard which had not been cut in years. I washed my hair and cleaned up the man bun. Then put on an outfit that Riley brought me a few months ago. It was a tailored dark blue suit, white dress shirt, brown cap toe dress shoes, designer belt, and a bow tie. I topped it off with the cologne she had got me for my last birthday. I was no longer going to bury myself. The caveman was gone.

When I walked downstairs, I watched as everyone's jaw dropped to the floor. Riley exclaimed, "Pierce!"

"Take a picture, it will last longer." We all busted out laughing.

"Wow Mr. Kennedy. Who did you swap bodies with," said Emily?

"Thank you, Emily," I replied with a grin on my face.

"You look good dad," said Junior. I walked up to him and gave him a high five.

"Thanks buddy."

"Well, Prince Charming. We should head out," said Riley.

"Yes madame. After you."

I must give it to Riley because she was really trying. Most of the ride we had small talk about random things going on, but it did not seem forced. I actually was enjoying her company.

When we arrived at the restaurant, she had the SUV valet. She did not want her "hundred thousand dollars" vehicle possibly getting scratched in the lot. My first impression of the restaurant was that it looked amazing. It could have been rated six-stars. It was even better when we walked inside. I turned to Riley and said, "This place is packed. I'd be surprised if there is an open seat."

"I made arrangements earlier. There are benefits to knowing the right people," she proudly replied.

The restaurant was in Gaslamp Quarter and the owner was Nina Williams. She was often referred to as the Queen of San Diego. She was in her thirties and apparently grew up in the city. I had heard she had got her start being the muscle for cities the previous big-time drug lord before moving into the drug game herself. Nonetheless, she was easy on the eyes and did not come off as harsh as the stories about her suggested.

However, that was all speculation and she was the woman. She had a powerful persona that demanded respect. She put on a good front in public but, we all knew what her main source of income was. Nevertheless, she was still one of the most adored people around. There were politicians, street guys, law enforcement, corporate guys, celebrities, and everyday citizens all showing her love. Everyone praised her when they were in her presence. Many people were fond of her, but she was also hated by some. There was always a family member or friend accusing her of providing the drugs that killed their loved ones, but it didn't matter. She had the right people on her side to discredit those accusations and make them go away.

She happened to be at the restaurant that night hanging out with professional football players for the LA Cougars Lamar "L.J." Jenkins who played wide receiver and Derrick Wright who played safety. I watched her every move like everybody else in the restaurant. She was not even doing anything but was still the center of attention.

As we were seated the waiter approached me and Riley. "How are you folks doing tonight?" Then he gave us our menus and a rundown of the specials. Afterwards he asked, "Can I start you off with some drinks?" Riley ordered a glass of water with lemon and I had the same. After the waiter took our order and left Riley said, "I should have ordered a bottle of wine." I tried to stop him, but it was to no avail. He was already at another table. As I was getting up, she stopped me. "Don't worry about it. I'll ask when he comes back."

Shortly after Mayor John Wallace walked over to us and said, "Hey Riley I thought that was you." She turned to him and they shook hands.

"Good evening Mayor Wallace. I see we're not the only ones looking for something good to eat tonight." He laughed.

"This is the best place in town."

"John this is my husband Pierce." He extended his arm out and we shook hands.

"So, you're the lucky guy. Pleasure to meet you. My wife Cheryl is seated at the table already with our daughter. Let me see if I can get her attention." He looked in her direction and waved his hand. He caught her attention and once she waved, we all waved back.

Before he could start talking again, I excused myself from the table. "I have to run to the bathroom. Nice to meet you Mayor. Have a great night and enjoy your meal."

On the way to the bathroom I heard a raspy voice say, "Yo Pierce." I looked back but I did not see anyone I recognized. Then I heard, "Over here." In the corner of my eye I saw a hand waving, but I was still unclear of who it was. The lights in the restaurant were dim which did not help my bad vision. As he approached me, I got a good glimpse.

"Hey James, how are you doing?"

"You clean up well my friend. I am Great. Yourself?"

"Thanks. I am good. What are you doing here? I thought you had a family get together."

"Yea, I do. The owner Nina is my aunt, so we decided to have it here."

"Aunt? Aren't you two almost the same age?" He laughed.

"Yea, she's two years older than me. To make a long story short my parents had me early and my grandparents had her late."

"Oh okay. Why do you put up with a job at Dash with an aunt like that?"

"She may be rich but I'm not, so I got to punch the clock."

"Understood. Well I do not want to hold you up. Enjoy your evening. I'll see you at work."

"Likewise. If you need anything while you are here,

just let me know." I nodded my head.

"Thanks." We shook hands and as we parted ways, I stopped him and asked, "Now that you mentioned it. Can you have some Pinot noir sent to my table? I want to impress my wife." He smiled.

"No problem. I'll make sure you're taken care of."

I walked into the men's room and peed. When I was done washing my hands the bathroom employee handed me a napkin and said, "Your dapper tonight sir." I knew it was his job, but it felt good to be getting all those compliments that night.

"I think you're onto something." We both laughed.

I put five dollars in the tip jar, and he gave me two mints. As I looked around the room on the way back to my table, I was captivated by the beauty of the restaurant but more so by the story of the woman who owned it. This reinforced to me that the only thing that can stop you from doing anything is yourself. There is nothing that is unattainable if you want it bad enough. When I sat back down at the table Riley said, "There you are."

"Here I am."

"Someone sent us a bottle of wine. Compliments of the house."

While smirking and sipping on my water I replied, "There are benefits to knowing the right people." She laughed.

"You are something else Pierce Kennedy."

We went on to have a great evening and even better night. Riley can be a joy to be around when she tries.

Chapter VI

Street Queen (Nina)

This is the life. This is the reason why I have made so many sacrifices. Business is good and getting better. I stand here tonight with all these people surrounding me like I am the gift of life. Nonetheless, I am the hand that feeds them. They know not to cross me. I demand nothing but respect. My name is Giana Williams aka Nina.

The restaurant is packed and there is not one open table. Tonight, I will be hanging out with my featured guest L.J. and Derek. After dinner we will head over to my club (The Den) to talk business. For now, we will enjoy ourselves as the night is still young. Tonight, my parents, brother, sister in law, nephew James, his wife, Dame, L.J., and Derrick will all be celebrating my mom's birthday.

When my mom arrived at the table, I stood up to greet her. After we hugged, she took a step back and looked me up and down. "Nina, look at you. You are so beautiful. You should dress like this more often." Out the corner of my eye I could see Dame chuckling and I knew he was about to say something.

"Beautiful. I told her the same thing mama." I responded to his compliment with an elbow nudge then I directed my attention back to my mom.

"Thank you, mom."

Me and Dame grew up together in the same neighborhood. He always accepted and treated me like one of the fellas. Now he is my right-hand man. He is the main person who helps me keep my operation intact and his loyalty is unmatched. Together we are unstoppable. If I was not a lesbian, he might be my man. He is someone I can trust with my life and in this business that is hard to find. There is always an opportunist looking to stab you in the back. Especially, when you are a woman. On top of that I do not look like the typical drug dealer. I have silky smooth brown skin, long lustrous black hair that I usually wear in two French braids, a tight body, a lot of tattoos, and I do not take any shit.

When I looked over at the entrance, I saw L.J. and Derrick had arrived. They got held up talking and taking pictures with some fans. To be a celebrity you must pay your dues that is the price of fame. When they joined us at the table we were eating, drinking, talking, and having ourselves a good time. Shortly after the mayor came over to pay homage to me and my guest. I asked the waiter to pull up a seat for him and he said, "No need. I have my family over there waiting for me." However, I insisted.

"Lovely family. Take a seat, it'll only be a moment." I do not like people standing over me while I am sitting. It makes me uncomfortable. I continued on to say, "Are there any updates with our business?"

"So far everything is going according to plan. My guys did a test run with your supplier bringing in the merchandise and it was successful. Now it's up to you to deal with our friends across the border."

"I'll take care of them just make sure your guys keep delivering. I'll be in touch."

We continued enjoying our meal while celebrating mom's birthday. I topped the meal off with a designer handbag shaped birthday cake that was brought out by the waiter with sparklers. My mom loved her handbags. After singing "Happy Birthday" I gave my mom her gift. It was a handbag of course with a gift inside. When she initially got the bag, she looked at me and laughed. "How predictable."

"Look inside," I replied.

"What is it? A wallet?" She unzipped the bag and took out the box. She opened it and began crying tears of joy. Then she said, "Thank you baby it's beautiful." It was a four-carat diamond ring. That was the only ring I have ever brought for a woman. I try to be careful with the woman I allow in my life. After my mom got her gift, I said my goodbyes and told my family I had to run. Before we headed out, I told L.J. and Derrick to meet us at the club.

When me and Dame arrived at the Den there was a line wrapped around the block. I parked behind the building since I do not like to be seen when I enter or leave a place. I never know who could be watching me. We walked through the back entrance and made sure that everything was running according to plan. I walked over to one of my staff members and said, "Is the section set up for my guest?"

"Yes. It is all set. We're just waiting for them to get here," she replied.

"Good."

The success of my legit businesses will eventually help me get out of the life of crime. To be honest there is nothing different from how I make my fortune versus how corporate people do. We are all selling something whether it is viewed as good or bad for the people buying it. Our objective is to provide a service better than the competition and make a lot of money doing it. They just make laws against what I am doing because they do not control the business. Ironically, they benefit from this "dirty" money too. That is why they are all at my beck and call with hopes of getting a piece of what I have going on.

Me and Dame went into the office to roll up a blunt. It is the only drug that I will consider using. All that other stuff just kills you slow. Plus, I prefer to operate with a clear mind. We sat there reminiscing about old times and our future. Some time had passed and there was a knock at the door. It was Jason who was one of my best soldiers. His job was being my muscle. He let me know that L.J. and Derrick had arrived and were in their section. I had him bring them back to my office so that Me, L.J, Derrick, and Dame could talk business.

When L.J. walked in the room he said, "Nina it's a zoo in there. You did not tell me your club was off the chains like this. I would have been here sooner." I laughed and then got right to business.

"Listen fellas we all know why we're here. I have the supply and you have the demand. I know you guys came for some bud and that is cool, but I got something better. A real money maker." I watched as L.J.'s eyes opened with curiosity.

"And what is that?"

"China White."

"I don't know about that," L.J. replied.

57

"Yea. We are already taking a risk dealing weed. If we start messing with that it may draw some unwanted attention," chimed in Derrick. I could see that they were having doubts, so I decided to take a more direct approach.

"Look fellas. The streets are calling for it. Plus, I got a product that puts the shit on the streets to shame. Motherfuckers are dying for this shit. The pheens will be licking their chops and you will be one of the only people with a direct source. You'll make more in a couple months then in a season playing ball minus beating up your body." L.J. took a deep breath, turned his head to Derrick, and then looked back at me.

"If we were interested. How much are we talking?"

"For one key (kilogram) we're talking about a street value of three hundred thousand dollars."

"How much are we talking per key from you?"

"I only ask for a hundred thousand a key." They were still hesitant but by the look on their faces I could tell they were interested. With persistence I said, "What's it going to be fellas?"

"Wait. Aren't people dropping dead from that shit," replied Derrick.

"That's because they're getting junk. We have a real chemist behind our product. My supplier ensures me that will not be a problem for us. Regardless, the fact of the matter is the streets are calling for it. People dropping dead is actually good for business. It's free marketing." I watched Derrick as he shook his head side to side with uncertainty. Then I asked, "What's wrong Derrick?"

"We may need some time to think about it." I was beginning to get frustrated and responded with authority.

"We need to decide now. This is my offer." I shrugged my shoulders and pointed at a stack of money I had laying out on the table. I continued on to say, "This is what I'm about. I won't ask you again." They were still at a loss for words, so Dame stepped in.

"There's a bunch of guys lined up for this opportunity. We are bringing it to you two first because we fuck with you. So, do you guys want to take our business up another level or keep playing around with small change because either way we are taking a risk. We might as well aim high."

"Okay, we'll take it," L.J. replied. I looked over at Derrick.

"So, we have a deal?" Derrick put his head down and started rubbing his hands together for a few seconds before he looked at me. "

"Yea I guess so it's a deal," Derrick replied. We came to an agreement and all shook hands.

"Dame will go over the details with you later but for now let's go back to our sections and celebrate."

"I still want those twenty keys of bud too," L.J. replied.

"For sure. I got you."

I walked over to the door and opened it. Jason was waiting outside and took them back to their section. I approached Jason and said, "Make sure they get the best women available to accompany them and whatever they want to drink." He nodded his head in understanding.

"I'll take care of it."

Me and Dame stayed back in the office for a moment. When we were alone, I said, "This is our way into the LA market. This is going to make us enough money to do whatever we want. You ready for this right?"

"Come on man this is what we do this for."

I walked over to the cognac and poured us two shots. I gave him one and we made a toast. As our glasses collided, we both said, "Bigger than Life." We took our shots and gave each other a fist bump.

We went to our section and began to celebrate. In the moment I took the time to appreciate how far we have come. Dame has been nothing short of a blessing for me. As we partied in our section with four beautiful women. I caught myself and him making eye contact. In that moment we both knew it was more between us, but we have always kept it business. I have to admit when I was looking at him it was like we were the only two in the room. Nevertheless, I know I am tipsy so tonight I will blame it on the alcohol. We will be back to business in the morning.

Chapter VII

Ray (Riley)

While sitting in my office I thought back to last night. Me and Pierce actually had fun. We made up for some of the lost ground between us. I knew it would take time, but I had to work at it. I could not afford to have anything in my life out of place. I knew things were going to get hectic, so I did not need my personal life being a distraction.

All of the sudden I heard a vibrating sound and looked down at my cellphone on the desk. It was "Dad" calling me. Before I could answer the phone, my senior partner Martin Goldberg walked into the room. He asked me about a case we had coming up. It was with one of our major clients named Smith & Walton. They are one of the largest pharmaceutical companies in the U.S. They were facing criminal charges and thousands of lawsuits for promoting off-label uses of their product.

The product was an antipsychotic drug that was approved by the FDA to treat symptoms of bipolar disorder. However, they were promoting its use for conditions like ADHD. Unfortunately, the results of this decision have led to adverse effects for many of the individuals who have used it. These damages could cost the company millions if not billions of dollars. It would be a big hit to the company, but it was not like they did not have the money. Nonetheless, our job was to prevent it from getting to that point. My dad then texts me, "Call ASAP." I cut my conversation short with Martin and suggested that we meet with Jason Miller (CEO of Smith & Walton) for lunch.

I regrouped myself before calling my dad back so I could focus on the task at hand. He answered on the first ring and said, "Hey Hun. What did you think about the meeting with our partners?"

"Hey dad. I think it went well."

"Me too. I do not have to remind you how this changes everything for us moving forward. We would finally be legit. Do you understand what I'm asking of you?"

"Yes, I can handle my end. I'm working on it now."

"Okay. This deal is in your hands now. I'll send my associate and your brother to assist you with whatever you need."

"Do you think it's a good time to involve Ray?"

"Yea. He's ready now."

"The last time you said that things didn't turn out so good."

"Well, things change. Plus, I know you have no intent in being involved with the business outside of setting up this deal. I need someone I can trust to run the business for me, so you have to trust me."

"Right. When will they be here?"

"They'll be at the Cafe downtown that you like. Be there at one o'clock so you can brief them on what's going on."

"One o'clock. Today?"

"Yes. Today."

"A heads up would have been nice."

"This is your heads up."

Suddenly my office phone started ringing so I ended my call with my dad. It was Angela (receptionist) confirming the meeting with Jason at eleven thirty. I said, "That was quick."

"He was already in town for business."

"Of course."

"FYI, he sounded frantic."

"Duly noted. Thanks."

Luckily, both of the meetings were downtown and not too far from my office. I had a couple hours, so I took the time to prepare for the day. I immediately started looking over the case. I read the complaints, reviewed any copies of contracts between my client and plaintiffs, looked at witnesses, evaluated the strengths and weaknesses of the case, and prepared any useful documents. About an hour before heading out I phoned Angela to have Martin and a few other colleagues meet me in the conference room in fifteen minutes. In cases like this we like to collaborate in person before meeting with the client.

After developing the direction, we were going to take the case. We went to the Mexican restaurant in separate vehicles. While walking to my SUV that was parked in the garage, I sent a text to Samuel Smith (CEO of Masax) that read, "Hey Samuel. I have something I need to run by you. Do you have time to meet?" His company was the largest pharmaceutical company in the world. Coincidently one of their biggest sellers was an opioid pain medication called Maxadon. He owed me a favor for getting a bribery case against him dismissed a couple years ago in which I proved no quid pro quo. Now it was time for me to cash in on that favor. When I looked up, I found myself on the wrong garage level. I was on three, but I needed to be on four.

When I finally got to my SUV, I had a moment of Deja vu but of course this could not have happened before I have never had this type of pressure on me. It must have just been the stress. When I pulled up in front of the restaurant the valet took my keys and parked the SUV. Before walking inside, I received a video phone call from Junior. I looked through the window and could see Jason was already seated. I had some time, so I answered the phone.

"Hey mommy," said Junior. I smiled.

"Hey baby, Everything okay?"

"Yes, I'm okay, I just miss you."

"I miss you too. Aren't you in class?"

"We're on recess now."

"Is school okay?"

"Yea," he replied while being distracted by another kid.

Martin had arrived and as he walked by me, I told him, "I'll be right in." Then I turned my attention back to Junior.

"Baby you should go play with your friends. I'll see your afterschool mommy has to work now."

"Okay."

"Love you, Bye."

"Bye-Bye Mommy Love you."

When I entered the restaurant, I could see the frustration and unease on Jason's face. On top of that he was already on his third glass of whiskey. As I approached our booth, I greeted Jason, Conner (Jason's assistant), and Martin. When I sat down the waitress came over to take our orders. I asked for a variety of appetizers and a glass of water with lemon. Jason insisted everybody get a drink on him. I did not decline but I did not drink my glass. I do not like to indulge when attending work functions.

We started our conversation by opening the floor for Jason to express his concerns or questions he had about the case. His only question was if we could make it go away. He emphasized to us how the negative media attention was affecting his image and was bad for business. He also feared public scrutiny would lead law enforcement to make an example out of him. We assured him that we were prepared to deal with this case. We proposed the option of making civil settlements and paying the criminal fines. This would make the process much smoother and end it quicker.

Of course, he wanted to take the harder route. He insisted that giving in was admitting guilt. We reminded him of the odds stacked against us with the evidence and witnesses like the three whistleblowers from his own company. That did not seem to make a difference to him but by the end of the meeting he appeared to be more comfortable with the situation. Even though I was not sure if that was because of the alcohol or our counsel. Nonetheless, we were confident that we would figure something out. The meeting took around an hour which left me enough time to get to the cafe by one o'clock.

When I got to the cafe, I looked around the room for my lunch guest. They were not there yet so I got in line for a coffee. When I approached the register the barista said, "Can I get you anything?"

"Just a coffee, black no cream or sugar." That is when I heard the voice of my brother.

"And I'll have a blueberry muffin sis."

The barista asked, "Should I add that to your order?"

"Yes. That'll be fine."

"Coming right up."

After I received my coffee, I went over to sit with them. I gave Ray his muffin and the woman he was with said, "Did you order me one too?"

I awkwardly replied, "I'm so sorry. I didn't hear you say you wanted anything."

"Relax. I'm kidding." Then she extended her hand out to me and said, "I'm Kate by the way."

To be honest she was not at all what I expected. I had a hard time believing she was an associate of my dad. He was old school and she was unconventional. Her makeup looked as if it was done by a professional, she had a short blond haircut, with black leather pants, a blouse, and boots. I started to think my dad made a mistake. We shook hands and I replied, "I'm Riley. Nice to meet you. I have to say you look a little different then what I was expecting."

"Were you expecting an older woman, with glasses, a dress suit, and maybe a low bun." We laughed. Then she said, "If it's any consolation you're a lot hotter than I thought you would be."

I figured she was trying to hit on me, so I replied, "Look I'm not interested in women."

"Trust me you're not my type sweetie."

"Okay then. As you both know we're meeting today so I can brief you on my progress."

That is when I received a text from Samuel. It read,

"I'll be back in town in two days. Come by my Rancho Santa Fe house at seven o'clock pm. We can talk then."

"And you were saying," said Kate. I reoriented myself to our conversation and replied, "Sorry. I was saying that I will be meeting with a potential client in a couple days."

"Is there anything you need our help with to close this deal."

"No, I can handle it. I will let you both know when it is done. If I need anything, I'll be sure to let you know."

"Please do. I'm getting bored babysitting your brother." We all laughed.

"I see you got jokes Kate," Ray replied. I looked at my watch and saw I had needed to get back to the office.

"Well, I have to run. I will keep you updated on my progress. Until then if you need anything feel free to give me a call."

"Sure thing. We'll talk soon," replied Kate.

As I was getting up to leave Ray said, "Riley when can I see Junior?" I smiled at him.

"Soon."

Truth be told I was not sure. I loved my brother, but I needed to know that Ray was really committed to getting himself together. Otherwise I was not comfortable with him being around Junior. However, despite everything I had going on I walked out of the café ready for whatever lied ahead.

Chapter VIII

I am in (Pierce)

Two days after the shipment I was still feeling invigorated from the rush of living life on the edge. However, in the grand scheme of things my life had not really changed. It was still the same routine but my last trip to Mexico showed me there was light at the end of the tunnel. Before getting out of the truck I looked in the visor mirror and said to myself, "At least I got a chance to be a different guy for a day." I received a text from Riley that there was an envelope for me in the mailbox. I replied, "It's probably just junk."

"It's pretty thick and there's no stamp on it. Someone must have left it by the door for you." I was unsure why anyone would leave me mail.

"Put it to the side, I'll check it later."

I put the phone in my pocket and got out of the truck. Like always Mike and James were in front of the entrance taking a smoke break before the day started. I greeted them both but avoided any eye contact so I would not have to stop and talk. "Hey Pierce. Is everything okay," asked Mike.

"I'm good. Just trying to stay away from the secondhand smoke."

In reality I just was not ready to have those guys ruin my day. As I opened the door James said, "How was the wine?"

"It was nice. I appreciate it. I owe you one."

I went into the locker room and prepared for work like any other day. During the morning recap, I was surprised I was assigned to do the pickup across the border again. Usually we were on a rotation so that we only took one trip to Tijuana for each driver every week. Nonetheless I did not question the assignment. I got my documentation and did my vehicle inspection. I was actually thrilled to be going back despite the fact I almost shit myself the last time I was there.

When I arrived at the facility in Tijuana. Jose had a look on his face like he could not wait to tell me something. I was not sure if that was good or bad. He directed me to my dock and approached me as soon as I got out of the truck. "Hola mi amigo. Did you get your package? For your last visit."

"Package?"

"There was a package delivered to your house."

I thought to myself that must be the mail Riley was referring too. "How do you know where I live," I asked.

"Relax vato. My boss needed a little more insurance than just your word but that does not matter. We have more business to do together."

"Wait. That was a one time thing. Right?"

"I told you before there is no turning back. There is more business to be done. Besides why would you want to mess up something good. Do we still have an understanding?"

"Sure."

At the moment I felt like moving their product was better than their alternative option and it also felt good to be a part of something big. He put his hand on my shoulder and looked me in the eyes. "We need to discuss our arrangement moving forward in more detail." Then he turned around and said, "Follow me."

I tapped his arm and when he looked at me, I asked, "Why me?"

"Because you seemed like a guy I can trust, and I can tell you want more out of life. So, I gave you an opportunity." He continued walking and I followed him inside the building.

At first, I did not know how to feel. I thought to myself, "Why are we going inside of the office if we're trying to be discrete?" Then I realized this was bigger than Jose. Whomever was behind this was someone with real power. When we arrived in the office upstairs the room was empty. Jose pointed to the chair. "Please sit. My boss will be here soon." Those few minutes felt like an eternity. I had no idea of what to expect next. I was in the complete dark. It had already turned out Jose was not the average dock worker. Now he has got me caught up in some shit.

Suddenly appearing in the doorway was a short, rugged, and well-dressed man. My first impression of him was he did not look so scary, but he was clearly not your typical boss. He came in the room and sat down across from me. In a thick accent he said, "So your Jose guy from San Diego. I'm Miguel."

"Yes sir. It's a pleasure to meet you Miguel." I then extended my arm out to shake his hand. Initially it did not seem like he appreciated the gesture but after an awkward pause he reached out and reciprocated the handshake.

I could feel his eyes piercing through me as he analyzed my every move. He said to Jose, "Check him."

Jose patted me down thoroughly. I was so nervous even though I knew I had nothing to hide.

"He's clean," replied Jose. Miguel then turned his attention to me.

"Don't take this the wrong way, it's nothing personal." He walked toward the liquor cart and asked, "Would you like a drink?"

"No thanks."

"Good choice. You have to get our merchandise back safely. Do you know what our product is?"

"No."

"So, you didn't get a little curious during the first drop off and take a look?"

"Not at all. My job was just to get your product back to my facility." He laughed. He looked at the other guys in the room.

"See. This is a man who knows what to say. You two should take notes." Then he said to me, "Okay. To make sure there is a clear understanding between us we are going to go over how precious this merchandise is. The last load was ten kilos of heroin. You can't tell the difference between our merchandise and the candy companies you're already carrying." He had a box of candy on his desk and pointed at it before saying, "You didn't even notice the drugs right in front of you."

He was right, I did not. There was no way to tell the difference without opening it. He continued on to say, "This is basically pure gold that we're trusting you with. It is more valuable than your life." I just nodded my head in agreement. I knew this was hurting people and now I was a part of it. I figured it was the addict's choice to use it and now it was my job to make sure they got it. I knew if I made any mistakes that it could end badly for me. I finally came to the realization of what no way out meant.

I asked Miguel, "What is it you're asking of me exactly?"

"We only ask for your loyalty and that you get the job done. Other than that, we'll make a lot of money together cabron." We all laughed but I am sure we were laughing for two different reasons. I was so nervous I could have pissed my pants and he was just happy to have a mule for their product. He went on to say, "You'll receive payment based on the size of the load you move. This load will be ten times the size of your last. That is a hundred kilos and for this load will pay you five thousand dollars. That sounds fair right?"

"It sounds great but will the amount I'm carrying keep increasing or will it level off at some point."

"My bosses' goal is to move as much as he can. We will give you as much as we feel you can handle. Comprende?"

"Yes, but doesn't that make it more likely for me to get caught?"

"We have a major influence at the border and from what I understand you don't even have a single parking ticket so as long as you continue to do your job the way you've been doing there won't be any problems. Do not worry so much. When you get nervous it makes me nervous and that is not good for either of us. Moving forward Jose is who you will communicate with. Take his word as mine and if we need to talk at any point, I will get in contact with you." Then him and the other guy in the room walked out.

Jose looked at me and said, "It's official you're in mi amigo." I looked at him with a blank look on my face.

"I thought that was already established." He laughed.

"I wasn't sure how the meeting with Miguel would go but you held your own. If he did not like you. I don't know what would have happened."

As we walked back to the dock I was screaming in my head, "Fuck! This is real. What did I just do?" Before I got back in the truck, he pulled me to the side. "Moving forward there won't be any discussion of the product between us unless there is an issue. Our interactions will be casual. Your truck will be loaded during every delivery and you will go about it just like every other pickup. You will receive the payment in your mailbox two days after every drop off. It is as simple as that. Any questions?"

"No, it's pretty straightforward."

"You sure? If so, this is the time to ask."

"I'm good." We then shook hands and parted ways.

After the second trip the rush was just as invigorating. I wanted to maintain that high, so I sent a group message to Terry and Rich. The message said, "Let's meet up tonight at McSwiggan's Pub. I'm treating." I had not hung out with those guys in a while and I felt it was no time like the present to catch up. Shortly after I sent the message, I got a response from Terry that read, "I'm in." Followed by Rich agreeing to meet up too. The crew was finally getting back together. I knew they were surprised to see that I was the one initiating us all to hanging out. On top of that I was buying. I could tell the night was going to be epic.

When I got off of work I video called Riley. I made a silly face in the camera when she answered. "You are so stupid," she said as she laughed. Then she said, "I've

73

been thinking of some things we could do to build on the progress we've been making in our relationship."

"Sounds good. What do you have in mind?"

"We can have family game night tonight." She must have seen the disapproval on my face.

"What's wrong?"

"I love the idea you've come up with and we should definitely implement it in our lives."

"But."

"I have plans with Pierce and Rich tonight." To my surprise she did not make a fuss about it.

"Okay, this is sudden so I can give you tonight with the guys, but I need you to try moving forward."

"I will."

"I need you to promise me."

"Really? I think I've been doing a good job of proving how dedicated I am to making things better between us," I replied sarcastically.

"Seriously Pierce. Promise me."

I still was not sure about our relationship but if it could not be salvaged it was not going to be because of me. Riley and Junior were the most important people in my life. There was not anything I would not do for them. So, I promised.

I was so excited that night. I didn't even go home after work. I went straight to the bar that we were meeting at. I got there at seven thirty, so I had an hour to burn. I ordered an appetizer sampler, beer, and watched TV. It was on a sports news channel and the topic was drug use in pop culture. They were talking about the possibility of drugs like marijuana being legalized because of their medicinal benefits as an alternative to the current pain medications being used.

There were past athletes and entertainers in on the discussion talking about their tragic experiences with pain medications like opioids. Of course, now they were downplaying the usage of these drugs during this segment. I am no drug advocate myself, but I am sure these same drugs probably helped some of them mentally and physically continue to work and cope with their pain.

At eight thirty in came Terry and Rich. I waved my hand to signal to them where I was seated. I tried to wait for them to make it to the table, but I could not. I had to pee so bad I sprinted to the men's room. When I got back to the table Rich and Terry were staring at me. "What?!"

"Nothing man. You ran off like a bat out of hell. We didn't know what to think," Terry replied.

"Yea, when you took off, I was about to run out of here myself," said Rich.

They both started laughing hysterically. "Fuck both of you."

"How's things going? Looks like you got here early and already had a bit to drink," said Rich.

"I just figured it'll be easier to come here right after work."

"You didn't even stop home to take a shower or see your family first. What is going on brother," asked Terry?

"Everything is great. I just couldn't wait to hang out with you fools."

"Well, it's good to see you guys too," said Terry.

"Speaking of seeing you guys. What is up with you man. You look like a brand-new person. I almost didn't even notice you," said Rich.

"I know. When he came back from the bathroom and started walking toward the table, I was thinking who this douche bag is," added Terry.

"Don't hate the player. Hate the game." We all laughed.

"What made it even stranger is you wanting to go out and on top of that offering to pay. Something is definitely up with you," said Terry.

"He's right. What are you finally leaving Riley or something," added Rich?

"I just want to celebrate my promotion at work."

"Promotion to what? Truck washer," said Rich. They both laughed.

"You're an asshole Rich. No, I handle bigger loads for the company and that came with a raise."

"All jokes aside. Congrats. It looks like things are actually starting to look up for you. You finally cut that awful beard, combed your hair, and even got some money in your pocket. Does this mean we'll be getting the old Pierce back," asked Terry?

"I think so. I mean I feel good. It's like I'm finally coming into my own." Then I paused and said, "Watch it Terry. I do not ever say anything about your dreads. I had a great beard."

"Yea for a homeless person and don't talk about the dreads. I keep them nice. Ask your wife if she likes them," replied Terry.

"Whatever man." We all laughed.

"Speaking of Riley, how is she taking to the new Pierce? I feel like she liked the lap dog version," said Terry.

"Believe it or not. She seems to be all for it. We're working on us."

"That's funny. Carol proposed we do the same in our relationship," said Terry.

"If you think it's worth it. Try. Things have been a lot better at home for me as an individual and for us as a family. Plus, you have more to lose than me. Carol is a stay at home wife, she is pregnant, and you do not have a prenup. It would be cheaper to keep her." We laughed.

"You have a point," Terry replied.

"How's your girl Palmer doing," I asked Rich.

"Who is Palmer," Rich replied with a confused look on his face. Me and Terry both started laughing.

"Funny. You got me. Enough with all the mushy stuff. Let us all get some drinks. Waitress can we have three fireballs?"

"Coming right up," she replied. Rich continued to say, "I'm happy for both you guys but can we have fun tonight without a care in the world for old time sakes?"

We all took our glasses and gave a toast. Before we knew it. We were five shots deep. Even while tipsy I could not stop thinking about the trip to Mexico. Despite being excited about my opportunity for redemption. I actually felt a little guilty about being involved with an organization that sold drugs. I asked Terry, "What's your thought on people using drugs?"

"Why do you ask? Are you thinking about using it?"

"Not at all. They were talking about the impact of drugs specifically opioids being used for pain management by athletes and entertainers on the sports channel. I know you probably have patients that use them, so I was wondering what you thought about it."

"To be honest I'm probably not the best person to answer that question."

"What do you mean? You are a doctor. I can't think of a better person to ask."

"Yea some doctor. I am going to tell you guys something, but you cannot repeat this. Okay?!"

Me and Rich both replied, "Okay."

"I've been using pain medication scripts to make some extra money."

"Wait. Are you selling drugs," I asked in a low tone?

"No. I just make sure that my patients who need pain pills get them."

"That sounds exactly like something every drug dealer would say," said Rich.

"I think I'm just saying it wrong. To put it in context how it works is I charge my patients a fee of two hundred dollars for the visit and I write them a prescription for Maxadon."

"Are you crazy you could lose your license," I said.

"I won't. The visits are legit. Most patients have actual pain that needs to be managed and a few have developed addiction from being previously prescribed to help with an injury etc."

"It sounds risky," I said.

"It's better than letting them turn to the streets for drugs and getting a bad batch of junk. Depending on how you look at it I am doing good by my patients. Plus, I need the additional income to keep up with my current lifestyle because my base salary won't cut it."

"As long as you're doing it for the right reasons. Just be careful," said Rich.

Rich looked at it more optimistically than me but who was I to judge? I just delivered a truck carrying heroin across the border. However, he made a good point. Depending on your perspective it could be seen as a good thing.

I looked at my watch and it was eleven thirty. It was getting late. I received a text from Riley that read, "When will you be home?"

"Not sure. We're still here."

She responded back with a sexy picture and a message that read, "It's your loss."

I must have had a smile on my face while reading the message because Rich asked me, "What are you grinning about over there?

"Because of this text I received." Then I said, "It is getting late. I think I should head out."

"Are you kidding me. You want to let this night go to waste by going home early," asked Rich.

"What else did you have in mind?"

"Red Pumps (strip club). You two down?"

"I don't know. Things are just getting good at home. The last thing I should be doing is having another woman's titties in my face."

"Pierce don't be a buzzkill."

"You wouldn't understand Rich. You know what I mean right Terry?"

"I'm with Rich on this one. The night is still young." I looked at both of them with a smirk on my face.

"Two against one so I guess we're going."

"Yes! I knew you wouldn't let me down," exclaimed Rich.

I texted Riley, "Not sure when we're leaving but I'll be home right after." I got no response. I figured she might have fallen asleep or at least I hoped so.

We decided to drive our own cars and meet there. I made a quick stop at the gas station to get some mints and fill up my tank. I started thinking about how I never thought I would get back to the point of enjoying life. It was clear that whatever I was doing was working because it had been years since I had felt that good and I was ready to do anything to keep it that way.

When I pulled into the lot of the club. I parked in the corner, so my car was not visible from the road. We all walked in together and I decided to get us a private section. When we took our seats. A few of the dancers and the hostess approached us. I asked the hostess for a bottle of champagne while they were throwing money. As I was sitting down in the section a dancer seductively approached me. "Would you like a dance?"

"I don't know yet. What's your name?"

"Bonita."

"That's sexy."

"Just like you baby."

While she danced in front of me, I went to put a couple dollars in her g string, but I dropped it.

"Looks like somebody has been drinking."

"Just a little bit."

"Just a little bit my ass. I saw you stumbling when you walked in here."

"So, you were watching me?"

"Don't flatter yourself. It is my time on the stage. I'll be back."

I sat there smiling like a kid in a candy store. I watched her as she walked away. I thought to myself, "This is crazy. I barely even know her, and she has got me sprung."

I opened the champagne and drank straight from the bottle. When she hit the stage, it was all eyes on her. Especially my eyes. She was stunning. She could have easily been America's next top model. I salivated for her. She had beautiful brown eyes, long black hair, bow shaped full glossy lips, straight pearly white teeth, golden skin, and was shaped like an hourglass. It felt like I was living in a dream. The fact that we barely knew each other is what made that imperfect relationship so perfect. There were no strings attached. I get exactly what I need which is a moment to feel alive and have someone cater to me.

I looked over at Rich and Terry at the stage. They were both occupied and having a good time. After she got off stage she headed back up to my section. She asked if I would like a private dance. I agreed and she took me to a room in the back. The dances were twenty dollars a song and we danced for five. When she asked me if I wanted another dance I said, "Is it possible for you to do a little more?" Her smile turned to a scowl.

"Like what?!" I found myself in a situation I did not think I would ever be in. Asking for something I could get from my wife, but I wanted it from her.

"Slide that g string to the side and sit on my lap."

"I don't sell sex. If you're looking for that, find another girl!" I was drunk so of course I was persistent.

"I don't mean to disrespect you, but I want you so bad. I will pay double what I did for the dance. She remained firm on her stance.

"No!" I then found myself being desperate. I just wanted her to touch me. I was hard as steel and ready to blast off like a rocket ship.

"How about you use your mouth?" Her face cringed and I saw she was starting to get pissed.

"How about I just get them to kick your ass out for harassing me." Despite her rejection and serious demeanor. My desire for her grew uncontrollably.

"Well can you just rub it. I will pay you three times the amount. Three hundred dollars."

Looking at me with disdain. She was silent for a moment and did not say anything. I sat there hoping that meant she was considering it. "Okay, but only this once. I need the cash first."

"I have one hundred and fifty dollars on me. I'll run down to the ATM to get the rest of it." I could not believe I was going to blow three hundred dollars for a hand job. I was better off going home and jerking off but my hand was not hers.

When I got back to the private room, she was standing there with her arms crossed. "Do you have a condom? I don't want that stuff all over me."

"Yea, I do but do you at least have some oil."

"Yes, in my locker. Give me the rest of the cash. I'll be right back." She took the cash and went backstage. I could not help but think. She could literally just run off with my money. I mean I do not know anything about this woman other than her stage name. What was I going to say, "She took three hundred dollars from me for a hand job?" I said to myself sarcastically, "Yea, that would work out great for me."

She came back five minutes later. "Where's the condom?"

"I already put it on. I thought you might of took off on me"

"That is not how I get down. It is pretty dark in here, but we have to be discreet. Here is the oil put on the condom. I'll rub it while I dance on you."

When the next song began, I could not believe this was happening. I made the mistake of looking her in the eyes and the passion took over. I didn't even make it to the end of the song before I finished. She barely even touched me.

She chuckled and said, "That was quick. I need the money for dance too.

"I already paid you."

"No, you paid for the rub down. The dance is separate." She put her hand out and I gave her another thirty.

"Take your tip out of that. See you later."

"Thank your big tipper," she replied.

I was starting to sober up when I got back to the section. I was also starting to feel like the biggest fool. I thought to myself, "Did I really just do that?" I used to laugh at guys like me. Now I am the lame paying for sexual favors. Nonetheless, that night turned out to be one of the best I had with my friends. I sat back, grabbed the bottle of champagne, and enjoyed the entertainment.

Chapter VIIII

Progress (Pierce)

I woke up the next day to a text from Terry. It read, "If Carol asks you about late last night tell her we were out until this morning."

"No problem. Is everything okay," I asked.

After that no response. I figured he probably got himself caught up again. Nonetheless, it felt good to sleep in until ten o'clock. It was Friday and I had the day off of work and Riley had already taken Junior to school. Finally, I had time to digest what I have actually got myself into. I laid in the bed looking at the ceiling fan weighing the pros and cons. As I drifted into deep thought, I could hear the voice of Miguel echoing in my mind saying, "There is no turning back." It was engraved in my memory. I just needed to figure out how to live with it.

I had a session scheduled that afternoon with Dr. Shaw. I debated whether or not I should tell her about my promotion. I understood there was a doctor-patient confidentiality between us, but I did not trust her with that information. It was too risky. I had to be very careful with the information I shared. Nonetheless I was excited to talk to her about my progress. Maybe she would see I was actually trying to do better.

I felt like my old self again, so I skipped my

morning mirror exercises. In my mind I was cured and back to being me. I no longer needed those exercises. I was not going to skip breakfast though. I was starving. I opened the microwave to see if Riley left me anything to eat. When I opened the door, my eyes lit up. A steak and vegetable omelet. I was not expecting that, but I surely appreciated it. I turned on the microwave and started the coffee machine to get my morning cup to go along with breakfast. The coffee tastes like shit compared to the Frappuccino, but it got the job done.

After that meal, my belly was full, and I was satisfied for the day. I considered going upstairs and going back to bed, but I had to be at my appointment at twelve o'clock. I went into my closet and put on a gym outfit since me and Mikey were going to the courts later to play ball. When I exited the garage there was a sun glare that momentarily blinded me. I turned my head and pulled the truck visor down. I reached into my center console and put on my aviators. I had been looking for a reason to wear them and now I had one. While riding with them on with the music blaring, I felt like a star.

My psychiatrist was in University Heights so I figured I would text Terry again after my session since I would be near his home in Mission Hills. I walked into the office to sign in and I was greeted by her receptionist Abigail. She was a sweet woman and had a way of making you feel right at home. Each visit she greeted me like it was the first time I was there. I was fifteen minutes early and Dr. Shaw was wrapping up with another client, so I sat down and grabbed a magazine. It was rare that I actually looked at words on paper but for whatever reason I felt compelled to.

Of course, I picked up the weekly magazine that discusses nothing but gossip. As if I did not have enough crap in my own life to focus on. However, it was interesting and helped pass time. There was one story that caught my attention specifically. It was discussing the increasing numbers of deaths due to overdoses from opioids. It highlighted the use of fentanyl in the making of counterfeit Maxadon pills (street name maxy) and heroine. Despite the danger using the drug the popularity of it was growing. I continued reading it until Dr. Shaw called me into her office.

When I entered the office, I plopped myself down on her chaise lounge chair. She looked studious and was all business as usual. She was cute in her own way. That is why I even agreed to do therapy in the first place. How else can you sit in a room with a complete stranger and tell all your secrets if you cannot even stand to look at them. Attractiveness has a way of disarming me. It is a plus that she is actually smart and knows what she is doing. We had developed a relationship and I could see how the sessions were benefiting me. I kind of liked the opportunity to vent.

While I was getting situated on the chair she asked, "How was your vacation?"

"It was okay. Just like any other vacation."

"You were in Hawaii correct?"

"Originally it was supposed to be, but we changed it last minute to Hong Kong."

"It must have been real last minute because I saw you a week before you left. Has anything else changed? Other than cutting your beard." We both laughed.

"How do you like it doc?"

"It's nice. I actually know what you look like now."

"There actually has been some changes."

"Tell me about them."

"Well doc. I am starting to feel more like myself. I feel like I am getting support at home from Riley. I'm beginning to see that the only thing that was holding me back was me."

"Is there anything in particular that has sparked this change?"

"I feel like I hit rock bottom. It was time to change. It is like you said. I needed introspection. I needed to see myself for who I am. Then build on that."

"That's good. It sounds like you are taking a step in the right direction. What do you think you need to keep this going?"

"I feel like things are beginning to fall in place. Me and Riley are working on our relationship. Work has gotten better. Now I'm just taking it day by day allowing myself to continue to grow."

"What led to the change in your relationship?"

"Once we got back from the vacation it's like she had a change of heart. She wanted to do better by our family. I know that she said this before in the past, but her actions are actually aligning with her words."

"That's fantastic. I am happy to hear that. How's work going?"

"I just got a promotion."

"Congratulations. What is your new role?"

"I handle bigger loads for the company. It also came with a pay raise too. I'm actually being given an opportunity to advance."

"This is a sudden turn of events for you. It's good but we need to monitor this and continue doing the same things we've been doing."

87

The remainder of our session was mainly me talking and her listening. I walked out of there feeling refreshed. I had also enjoyed her praise of my progress.

When I got in my truck, I texted Terry again but still no response. Then I texted Mikey to let him know I was coming to pick him up to play ball. He lived fifteen minutes away in Lemon Grove. After I picked him up, we headed to Mission Beach Park. He could not wait to play. Mikey had a tremendous amount of energy. He was A.D.H.D. at its finest.

I knew Mikey was tapped into the streets, so I asked him, "What do you know about selling pills?" He laughed.

"Why what's up? Are you planning on becoming a dealer bro?"

"Not at all. I'm just curious about all the fuss about it."

"Well it's popular amongst drug addicts. If you haven't noticed there has been a rise in addicts around and that's the top dog on the streets."

"Do you know anyone who uses it?"

"My pops. That shit got him all fucked up."

"I feel you. My mom struggles with drugs too."

"It's fucked up, but people make their own decisions. And if they choose that life it is on them. Not me. Not you." I nodded my head in agreement.

"I hear you."

"But anyway, the dope boys love it. It pretty much sells itself. A guy I went to school with is making a killing now. He's always flashing the new shit he buys and stacks of money on social media."

"Have you ever thought about selling?"

"I thought about it, but it seems like the risk is

bigger than the reward. People either end up dead or in jail."

"You ever think that maybe that's because they're not doing it the right way?" He looked at me and smiled.

"Bro. What's up with all the questions. Are you thinking about getting in the game?"

"Nah man. The only game I'm getting in is the one on this court." As we approached the courts, he started clapping his hands.

"You ready to ball or what fool?"

"I'm ready, but are you?" He laughed.

"We'll see."

When we got to the courts. There were already people running full court on all the courts, so we sat down and waited for next. In one of the games there were two women on the court killing the competition. There was not one man out there that could guard them. They were hitting shots from everywhere and they looked good doing it too. They were doll face assassins.

However, there was one guy on the court who kept hacking and trash talking one of them. She was not feeding into it though. She just kept busting his ass but on one possession she crossed him and drove right by him. When she went up for the layup, he fouled her hard. When she got up, she was not happy. They got up in each other's face and an argument ensued. He actually had a nerve to push her first.

Everybody was trying to break it up. That is when she walked off and said, "I got something for him." I was not sure what that meant but she reached in her duffel bag and her friend grabbed her arm.

"No Nina not here. Let it go."

"Fuck that. This fool must not know who I am."
That is when I noticed it was Nina Williams. Luckily, her
friend stopped her because things were about to get
ugly. The others kicked the guy off the court and the
game broke up. When the game ended. Everybody was
giving the ladies their props for a good game. There
were a few haters but that is to be expected. Some guys
cannot accept the fact that a woman can play better than
them but not me. I give credit where it is due. I had to
give it up to them. I would have been impressed even if
they were men because they were true ballers.

After I gave it up to them, I asked the woman with
Nina, "Are you Pro?"

"Yea, I play for the LA Flames."

"What's your name. I'll check you out?"

"Naja Taylor."

"That's cool. Good luck this upcoming season."

"Thanks."

"Can I bother you for a picture while you're here?"

"Me too," said Mikey.

"No problem," she replied.

Then she gave my phone to Nina to take the picture.
When I looked at the picture, I was excited. She was the
first famous person I had ever met. I thanked her and we
shook hands. I took my and put it inside my duffle.
Then I knelt down to lace up my shoes. After that I was
ready to ball.

Chapter X

The Game (Nina)

My grandma always told me I deserved more than what we had growing up. That has always stuck with me whether I was on the basketball court, in the classroom, or running the streets. If I am going to do it. I am going to give it my all and be the best. I always hung around with Dame and his crew, but I did not get involved until about five years ago. That is when I earned my stripes being a soldier for the former San Diego Kingpin Lamont Jackson.

He is now doing a forty-year bid upstate. He was ruthless and taught me everything I know. Due to his blessing and the respect I earned putting in work with him. My transition to head honcho was smooth. I have no regrets and I would make the same decision again. This choice has changed my life for the better. My life has purpose now and I must do whatever it takes to hold on to it. Even if that means doing some of the most heinous acts like killing a person. At this point I am so numb to the things we do in this life. A hit on somebody is just like shooting a shot on the court.

My life has not always been this way though. Ten years ago, I was a freshman at San Diego College playing basketball. I made the All-Freshman, All-Academic and All-Conference teams my first season. The stage was set, and I was next up. Unfortunately, I suffered a ruptured Achilles the first game of my sophomore season and then I tore my ACL my junior season. I was not the same after that. When I graduated, I played overseas for a season, but I was homesick and eventually gave it up. Now I just play pick up when I have time to run. Today me and my girl Naja just got done trashing these guys at Mission Beach. It still feels good to play. Especially, when you get love from those who respect your game. Following the game, we sat on a picnic table by the court and talked a bit to catch up.

"That was a good run," said Naja.

"Yea it was. Just like old times. I needed that. It has been a while. I could of went without that punk fucking with me though."

"Jerk. I'm just happy I stopped you."

"Oh, he is too." We laughed.

"You're crazy. You haven't been balling?"

"I'd like to play more but I haven't had time lately. Been too busy."

"Oh, is there someone special in your life?"

"Yea me, myself and I." We laughed.

"That's no fun."

"We can't all be as lucky as you and find somebody like your man Keith."

"Yea you're right I am lucky," she said jokingly. We laughed.

"Plus, I wouldn't want to expose anyone to the life I live."

"Right. What are you up to now?"

"Just working."

"Just working huh. Well just be careful. I don't want to see you caught up in some dumb shit."

"I try my best to stay out the way. So far, it has been

working."

"Let us keep it that way. How have you been outside of that?"

"Business is good and about to get a lot better."

She pointed at my ride and said, "I see that. I peeped all the jewelry and your decked-out sedan when you pulled up

"Hey, I'm just trying to keep up with you." We laughed.

"Seriously. Are you good?"

"Yea I'm good. I got money in my pocket, a home to lay my head, and food to eat. I cannot complain. Plus, once we make a few more moves. We can leave the streets alone and go straight legit."

"You really think so?"

"It has to work out that way. I am in too deep. I got to move forward with it."

"I hope I'm right. I'm going to pray for you." I smiled.

"Thanks. I need it but enough about me. Are you ready for your upcoming season? Because your left hand looked a little weak out there." We laughed.

"Now you know I don't have to get ready because I stay ready."

"For real. I feel that."

"Well, I have to get out of here. It was nice seeing you. Let us do this again. Sooner than later"

"No doubt."

"Stay safe. I will see you later."

"Will do. Later."

I sat there a little longer by myself just looking at the ocean and thinking about how peaceful it was. Sometimes I get so caught up in all of the commotion going on around me. I do not take time to appreciate the beauty right in front of me. I got a text from Dame saying, "We're all set. I'll be by in half." He was referring to the deal with L.J. and Derrick. He would be by my place to make the cash drop off after. I only lived fifteen minutes away in the Marina District. I had a penthouse that overlooked part of the city and the ocean. It was my own little castle.

As I was looking out onto the city from my penthouse still wearing my sweaty clothes. I heard the elevator and knew it had to be Dame because I just told the doormen to allow him up when he arrives. When he entered the room I said, "What do you have for me?"

"I got the bag. It is all there. Five hundred thousand dollars for the china white and sixteen thousand for the bud."

"Great work." I did not feel a need to count it. I knew Dame would not ever try me that way, so I put the bag off to the side.

"Would you like a drink?"

"Yea, I'll take one." I poured a glass of cognac and passed it to him.

"You're not drinking with me?"

"Nah, I'm already dehydrated from balling earlier."

"Where'd you ball at?"

"Mission Beach with one of my old teammates. She was nearby so I took the opportunity to lace up my balling sneaks."

"Which teammate?"

"Naja Taylor."

"Naja Taylor on the LA Flames?"

"Yes, that Naja Taylor."

"I didn't know you two were that close. You need to

bring her fine ass by the club." I was not hardly about to have Naja hanging around us when she had a good thing going for herself, so I just changed the subject

"Maybe. What's on the agenda for tonight?"

"The usual. Make sure all the sets are doing what they are supposed to be doing. Then go by the restaurant and end up at the club. Are you sliding tonight?"

"Nah, I'm going to chill tonight. I am sore. I will circle back tomorrow. Call if you need me." He finished the glass and put it on the counter.

"For sure. Thanks for the drink." I stopped him as he was starting to walk out.

"Before I forget to be at the club by seven in the morning. There's something we have to take care of so don't be up all-night fooling around and talking about you overslept." He smirked and made a face at me.

"You keeping tabs on me now? Do not worry. I will be there. Later."

After he left, I was starting to cramp up, so I made a run to the convenient store to get a sports drink. As I was entering the store, I saw the guy who was talking shit earlier at the courts leaving out. I felt like now was a good time to settle the score. I followed him until we were in an area where I could confront him without any witnesses. Yea, I thought about what Naja said earlier about letting it go but I could not. I had a reputation to protect and there was no way I could let someone disrespecting me go unpunished. She did not understand street justice. On the other hand, I know that Dame would say I am letting my pride get in the way of business. However, to me this is business and I had to take care of it. As a woman you had to demand respect

95

or dudes will try to walk all over you. I got the name "Nina" for a reason. I let my gun talk for me.

Once he went into the alleyway. I ran up behind him and pushed him against the wall. I pointed my gun at his head and said, "Put your hands up against the wall." He quickly put his hands up and started to panic.

"What do you want? I don't have anything." I could tell he was terrified.

"Oh, you don't remember me. Turn your bitch ass around." While my hand was on his back, I could feel his body trembling and heart pounding. He turned around slow. When he looked at me his eyes opened wide like he had seen a ghost.

"You," he mumbled.

"Yea it's me. What is all that shit you were saying earlier? Why don't you say it now?"

"Please. I did not mean anything by it. I was just talking trash."

"No, I think you did." He held his head down and kept shaking it side to side.

"No words for me now huh?"

"What do you want me to do to make it right?"

"Apologize!"

"I'm so sorry. We were just playing ball." His apology was not enough. The anger inside me of me just took over and I could not forgive him.

"Yea, you are sorry." I shot him in the head. Boom! I watched as his body folded and fell straight to the ground. Afterwards, I ran off, wiped the gun down with my shirt sleeve, and tossed it off the pier. Like I said the streets have changed me. I was going to survive and be successful by any means necessary.

Chapter XI

The Meeting (Riley)

What a day. Now I had to pull myself together to meet up with Samuel. I had already told Pierce I was going out with a client for work tonight. Good thing he does not question me anymore. It would make this process that much harder. He did ask me why I was wearing jeans tonight. I usually wore dresses, but this meeting was more casual. I wore black jeans, leather ankle boots, and white roll-up sleeve hem blouse.

Before I left, I kissed Junior and told him, "Goodnight." Then I said to Pierce, "Don't wait up for me. I am not sure how long this meeting will be. I may get in a little late." I kissed him and said, "Bye." As I walked to my SUV. I got a text from dad that said, "Call me after the meeting."

When I arrived at the residence there was a gate. I rang the bell and a man said, "How can I help you?"

"I'm here to meet with Samuel."

"And your name is?"

"Riley."

He opened the gate and said, "Pull into the driveway and park." It was a huge estate with magnificent landscape, and it was on the side of the hill overlooking the beautiful mountainous terrain. When I got out of my SUV I was greeted by a man in a black suit.

"He's waiting for you inside. Right this way." I followed him into the house and sitting in a side office room was Samuel.

When I entered the room the man in the black suit shut the door behind me. Samuel said, "There you are. How are you Riley?" He extended out his arm and we shook hands.

"I'm good. Yourself."

"I'm good. Thanks for asking." I looked around his room admiring his decor.

"You did a fabulous job decorating this office." He laughed.

"Thank you but the only thing I did was pick a great interior designer." Then he offered me a seat.

"I appreciate you taking the time to meet with me. I know you are a busy man so let me direct. I asked you to meet with me to discuss a business opportunity that could be mutually beneficial for both you and me."

"You're ready to get right down to business. I can appreciate that but what do you know about the pharmaceutical business."

"I'm not just a lawyer. My family and our partners have been successful in the business for a long time overseas."

"Okay. I'm listening."

"Make us as your API manufacturer. We can provide you with the best price, quality, and a supply that will guarantee you won't ever have any shortages." He took a deep breath.

"I'll talk to the board and see what they think."

"Look don't bullshit me. You are the majority shareholder. What you say goes."

"I don't work like that. I cannot just bring on an API manufacturer. There's rules and regulations that must be followed. You know that."

"I do. I also know that your drug Maxadon is patented so you have exclusive rights to how the drug is manufactured. As far as getting approval from the necessary national health officials I'll take care of that." Then I paused for a moment and said, "I forgot to mention one thing. You owe me this favor, so I won't take no for an answer."

"Favor? I thought you were just doing your job. After all you are my lawyer."

"Yes, and now I'm your partner."

"You may be in luck. We have been having some issues with our current supplier."

"We can help you with that. Give us a chance." As an act of agreement, I put my hand out and he reciprocated the gesture.

"You drive a hard bargain, but you have a point. No wonder I hired you."

"I assure you this will be profitable for us both and it will make your life much easier. So, are we in agreement?"

"We are. As long as your business can meet our expectations and you handle all the necessary legal stuff." Then he let go of my hand and said, "I've prepared a meal for us. We could talk more integral details over dinner." I followed him out to his dining area where he had a large meal spread with servers catering to us. It felt like we were eating a thanksgiving meal at a five-star restaurant. When I sat down, he asked, "Please raise your champagne glass to toast our new partnership." We toasted and that marked the beginning of our business together.

I ended up leaving Samuels around ten o'clock. On my way home I called my father to share the news. When he answered I said, "It's done. We will be an API manufacturer."

"Remarkable. I knew I could count on you," he enthusiastically replied.

"I just need to handle a couple more things on my end and we'll be ready

"Sounds good. Do you need anything from me?"

"No. I'm good for now. I just wanted to keep you updated."

"Okay. I will let our partners know. Talk to you later Hun bye."

Convincing Samuel to commit was the easy part. Getting the FDA to speed up the regulatory requirement process and approve us was the hard part. Fortunately, Martin played golf with the FDA Commissioner Dr. Jacobs on Saturday mornings at a private course in Torrey Pines. I knew where to find him, but I needed to figure out how to convince him to help me. I felt like this was the first time I would have to get my hands dirty but what does it matter everybody's hands are dirty. Sadly, that is how it is. You have to pay to play.

Martin always asked me to come out and play golf with him, but I would always find an excuse not to. Truthfully, I find the game to be boring. I do not understand why anybody would waste their time playing it. Needless to say, I was finally going to take him up on his offer. Before I went to bed, I texted him a message that read, "See you on the golf course tomorrow morning (smiley face)."

I woke up the next morning to my phone ringing. It

was Martin. "Hey Riley. I just read your message this morning and given how late it was I figured I'll give you a wakeup call."

"Much obliged. Where should I meet you at?"

"We'll be at the country clubhouse at eleven o'clock. You can meet us there. By the way what has led you to the change of heart about golf?"

"I figure it's a skill that will come in handy especially since most of our clients play. So, who better to learn from then a pro like yourself?" He laughed.

"I'm not hardly a pro but thanks for the compliment. Anyways I will see you at the course. Bye."

When I arrived at the clubhouse Martin introduced me to the three other men we would be playing with. The first thing Dr. Jacobs said to me was, "Hey Martin I didn't know you had such beautiful colleagues." Then he grabbed my hand and kissed it.

"Thank you," I replied. I figured well at least I do not have to get him to like me. It appeared just my mere presence took care of that.

After playing horribly for a couple rounds Dr. Jacobs offered to help me with my swing. Shortly after I made a birdie. I turned to him and said, "Thanks."

"Anything I could do to help just let me know." He was such a flirt and making this a lot easier.

"Actually, there is something else you could help me with," I replied in a sexy tone. He came closer to me.

"Is that so."

"It is. I just completed paperwork for an API manufacturer that I'm partnered with and from what I understand the process could take a while but I figure that if you look at it for me personally the process could move much faster."

101

"That's right," he replied arrogantly.

"If you did that it would be much appreciated."

"And how would I know that?" "You'd know. I would be sure to show you," I replied seductively.

"What do you have in mind?"

"What would you like?"

"How about you come over to my place after this game."

"Well as tempting as that sounds. How about we consider that after you approve my company. For now, we can agree upon a payment of fifty thousand dollars."

"Are you trying to bribe me?"

"Of course not. It is going to get approved anyway. I simply just want to share the money I will save from you speeding up the process. While also considering coming over pending the expedited approval of my company." He smiled and grunted.

"I'll take a look at it for you." The rest of the group had already moved onto the next hole.

"Are you two going to join us," asked Martin?

"We're on our way," I replied. Now I had everything in order for the plan to be executed. I left the golf course prepared for the unknown challenge ahead.

Chapter XII

Day Trip (Pierce)

I went to sleep alone and woke up with Riley beside me. She must have had a long night because she usually got out of bed before me. I went downstairs and decided to make breakfast. I wanted to spend the day together as a family. I made cinnamon pancakes, scrambled eggs, sausage, and yogurt with fruit. Of course, I made coffee as well. I checked the mailbox and there was my package. I opened it up and there it was five thousand dollars. I could not help but think what they were making if this was my cut.

I went on my laptop and searched the street value of heroin and opioid pills. I not only wanted to understand the market but also the actual drug. An article written by a popular journalist and reporter named Wendy Summer talked about the devastation it had caused to communities and the fortunes drug dealers were making off of others' pain. The allure of the potential profit was stronger than the drug itself. I looked at the five thousand on the table and thought about going into business for myself. But How?

I heard someone coming down the stairs, so I logged off the computer and put the package on the side of the couch. It was Riley. I greeted her with a hug and kiss. Then asked her, "Late night last night?"

"Sure, but everything worked out good."

"Great. Today I want to do something for you and Junior." She grinned at me.

"Is that so."

"Yea. You both deserve a day to relax and have fun. With my promotion things have been going well. So, for once I want to spoil you both."

"I would love to be spoiled. I am in and you already started the day off right with making breakfast. Thank you hunny." We had a vibe again. It felt like old times. This was the Riley I loved. I did not want to lose her again. I was still optimistic though. I did not want to get my hopes up just yet. She asked, "Did Junior wake up yet?"

"No, I'll go get him so we can eat." When I walked into his room. He was not in the bed. I said, "Hey Junior are you in here buddy?"

He replied with a gargled, "Yea." He was already in his bathroom brushing his teeth. It was funny how during the week he had a hard time waking up but, on the weekends, it was not a problem.

"Come downstairs when you're done to eat breakfast."

I was not sure where to take them, so I figured I would let them decide. When Junior joined us at the table. We said our grace and dug in. The first thing out of Juniors mouth when he bit his pancakes was, "Mmmmmm." Me and Riley looked at each other and laughed. I asked Junior, "What would you like to do today?" He responded with a shoulder shrug. Then I said, "So you can't think of anything?"

"Well, I would like to play some video games and go to the beach."

"Okay, I think we can make that happen. And you Riley?"

"I'd like to relax on the beach. It's the perfect day for it." I suggested that we go to Mission Beach. That way we could play some games on the boardwalk and go to the beach after. They were both excited about it. Riley even promised not to do any work the whole day. When we finished eating, we all went upstairs, got dressed, and packed a day bag.

The ride to Mission Beach was smooth. We sang songs during the short drive. When we got there, it was busy. It took some time to find a spot but once we got our parking situated, we hit the boardwalk. It was seventy-eight degrees and sunny. The perfect day. The first thing we did was go to the arcade. We were all really competitive, so it made it fun. Most of the time Riley was destroying us in all the games. There were a few she let Junior win, but she did not let up on me. Especially, on air hockey. We were at it for hours. It was a blast. Before we left, they both wanted to ride the roller coaster. I hate heights so I waited outside. I watched as they began yelling as the ride came thundering down. I thought to myself, "Damn I don't know how they do it."

Out of the blue a guy stood next to me and said, "I got something that will take you on a better ride than that roller coaster." I looked to my left.

"What?"

"I got bud, blow, whatever you need."

"No thanks. I'm good."

"Oh okay. Let me guess you like to party. I got that too." I was starting to get annoyed but before I told him to fuck off. I thought maybe this could be my chance to find a pill supplier.

"Do you have any maxy?" Good thing he was not a cop because I would have been busted.

"Yea I got you. How many do you need?"

"I'll take one."

"That'll be twenty."

"Cool." After I handed him the money, he swiftly handed me the pill.

Before he could walk away, I asked, "How is the price determined?"

"Fool. What do you think this is street drugs 101?"

"My bad. If I need more. How do I get in contact with you?"

"Hurry up and take this number down. It is 555-555-5555 and the name is J-Money just hit my line. No texting."

"Okay. I am P. I'll be in touch."

He left just as Riley and Junior were getting off the ride. I hurried and put the pill in my pocket. When Riley approached me, she said, "Are we ready?"

"We sure are my love." She laughed.

"Are you okay?"

"Never been better." Before we hit the beach, we stopped at a taco stand and got a few chicken tacos. We loved Mexican food and that taco stand had some of the best in the area.

Prior to stepping in the sand, we took off our flip flops and raced to the water. Just before getting in the water I remembered I had something in my pocket. I told them, "Go ahead without me. I'm going to set up a spot for us on the beach." While I laid under the umbrella, I watched Riley and Junior as they played in the water. I held the pill bag in my hand and stared at it. I asked myself, "Is this the answer to my prayers?" I was convinced it was, but I would not be able to do it alone. I needed help. Someone I could trust but I could not ask Rich or Terry.

However, there was someone else I had in mind. Mikey was always looking for a way to make money. I just had to figure out how to get him on board with it. Nonetheless, I was not going to figure it out today. I put the pill in my bag and ran out toward the ocean to join my family.

We were tired by the time we left the beach. They both fell asleep during the drive home. Meanwhile, I was racking my brain trying to figure out a way to cover my operation. During the drive home I saw a sign for Seductions Strip Club in the Midway District. They were having a going out of business party. The best yet craziest idea I had ever fell right into my lap. A strip club would be the perfect cover up for drug distribution and laundering money. Also, with the business hours I would be able to keep my job. Now I just needed to get me a partner and a club.

Chapter XIII

All Hands-on Deck (Pierce)

Yesterday was fun and definitely needed. Our household moral could not have been higher. My future had not felt that promising since I was accepted to Medical School. To get my day started I needed to see if Emily could watch Junior on such short notice why I handled some business. Luckily, Emily was able to babysit at three o'clock.

While I waited, I looked up Seductions Strip Club and found the real estate company who had it listed as rent or buy. The agent's name was Tom Smith. I called him and scheduled a meeting that day at four o'clock. Then I called Mikey immediately after and asked, "Are you available at three thirty?"

"Maybe not sure. I may have to train a client then."

"Well postpone it. I have a business proposition you'll want to hear."

"What are you talking about?"

"Just be ready at three thirty. I'll be by to pick you up."

"Alright, this better be good. I'll be missing out on money."

When the clock struck three o'clock the bell rang. I opened the door and as Emily came inside the house I walked out.

"Nice to see you too," she said sarcastically.

"Sorry. Good morning. I am in a rush. Thanks for coming over in such short notice."

When I got to Mikey's house, I texted him, "I'm here." I waited a couple minutes and still no response. I hoped he was not flaking out on me. Then I called him, and he answered. "I just texted you. Are you ready?"

"My bad bro. I fell asleep. I'll be right out." He came out a couple minutes later rubbing his eyes.

When he got in the car, we shook hands and I said, "What's up."

"So, what do I owe this pleasure?"

"I got a way for us both to make some money."

"How?" I showed him the pill.

"Nah bro. I am good. I don't use pills."

"It's not for us to use. It's for us to sell."

"So, you're a drug dealer now?"

"No, we are." He laughed

"You are full of surprises Pierce. What are you having a midlife crisis or something?"

"I'm serious about this. There's a lot of money in this business. Drugs have fucked up my life enough. It's time it makes it better."

"You don't know the first thing about selling drugs."

"That's why we should be partners. You know the streets and I got the funds to get us started." He shook his head and looked straight ahead at the windshield.

"I don't know. I've seen a lot of people get fucked up in this game."

"I have a plan."

"Everybody who starts has a plan."

"Not like mines. Mikey this could work."

"How long have you been thinking about this?"

"Not long."

"Clearly. What's your plan?"

"We're going to use a strip club as a cover up. It will be easy to clean the money and we could distribute it out of the club. No street corner shit. I already have a contact for the pills. I just need a partner."

"Damn Pierce this is some heavy shit. You think we could really pull this off."

"Look I have a meeting set up with the real estate agent in thirty minutes for the building. I am giving you a chance to stop living session to session and make some real money. You down?" He looked me in the eyes and stared for a moment.

"You're serious?"

"As a heart attack." He took a deep breath and exhaled.

"Fuck it. Let's go."

"That's what I'm talking about!"

The way to the club was quiet. We both knew we were risking a lot to do this. When we were close Mikey said, "Oh snaps. Seductions. This was my spot when I was sixteen. They never carded us. I had some good times there."

"And there will be many more to come. I think that's him right there." Sitting on the hood of a red sports convertible was a well-dressed man. We approached him and I said, "Tom."

"Pierce? Nice to meet you."

"Likewise. This is my partner Mikey." He shook both of our hands and pointed at the club.

"So, what do you think of the building?"

"It looks like it's in good shape and it's a nice size."

"It's about ten thousand square feet. The previous owner took good care of it too."

"Why's the previous owner leaving?"

"Let us just say he's a great promoter but a terrible businessman. Do you plan on having the same type of business?"

"Yes. I do."

"Okay. Let us check out the inside gentleman. Right this way."

When we got inside Tom said, "It's early but this can give you a feel of what it's like here."

It was not too busy however I noticed that some of the guys there were military men. I figured it was probably because the naval base was not too far away. Nevertheless, I felt that they may be good for business. Law enforcement would not want to bust a place full of servicemen. For that reason, they may turn a blind eye to this place.

Then I looked on the stage and there was a woman that took my breath away. She was gorgeous and the way she moved on the stage was mind blowing. I tapped Mikey on the shoulder and said, "She stays." We laughed.

"That's your call. You'll be the boss," Tom replied. He continued to take us on a tour of the rest of the building. Since the owner was not there, we met in his office to talk numbers.

Tom asked, "What do you think of the place?"

"It'll work."

"Yea, it's just how I remembered," added Mikey. We all laughed.

"So, it's what you were looking for," asked Tom?

"It is but what's the cost of a place like this," I

replied?

"Well if you're looking to buy it. The asking price is 1.1 million dollars."

"That may be out of my price range."

"Well we would be only asking for ten percent upfront. Which is about one hundred and ten thousand dollars. You could get the rest in loans."

"I could get that eventually but at this moment that's still a bit steep."

"No worries. There is another option. You could just rent it for five thousand a month. You'll need insurance for the property, a strip club permit which would be another five thousand dollars, and a liquor license if you plan on serving alcohol." I pulled ten thousand dollars and cash out of my bag and put it on the desk.

"Perfect. Where do I sign."

"We generally don't take cash, but I'll make an exception today." We all smiled and shook hands. Then he said, "We just need to fill out some paperwork and do a credit and background check after we finish up here today."

"No problem." I was fine with that. I had no debt since Riley paid off all my school loans. After completing all the paperwork. He let me know the place would be mine in two weeks. Afterwards, we went out to the bar and all got a drink together. The girl I saw on the stage earlier walked by me and I had to say something.

I grabbed her hand and said, "Excuse me. How are you doing? My name is Pierce." She aggressively pulled her hand away.

"And."

"I'm sorry I don't mean to offend you but I'm going

to own this place in a couple weeks, so I wanted to introduce myself."

"Hi, I'm Secret. I have to get back to work." She was sassy and I liked it. When the light hit her face, I noticed it was the woman I hung out with at the bar.

"Natalie! You don't remember me from McSwiggan's?"

"Wow. I do. How are you," she replied in amazement?

"I'm good."

"I'm sorry about the attitude. It's been a rough couple days for me."

"No worries. I hope you'll really consider staying."

"I just might now. I have to get back on the stage. We will catch up later. It was nice seeing you." I thought about that night we had together from time to time and often wondered what I would do if given the chance to be with her again. I felt maybe now I would get the chance to put that thought to the test.

When we left and got back in the car Mikey said, "You weren't bull shitting."

"No, I wasn't," I arrogantly replied. The only thing I needed to do now was get connected with J-Money. I dropped Mikey off and said, "I'll be by after work so we can talk more about our business."

"For sure. Be safe. Later."

Before pulling off I called J-Money. He answered and said, "What's up?"

"It's P. I need that thing we were talking about at the beach."

"I don't know a P."

"We did business yesterday at the beach. I told you I'd be in touch." He paused for a moment.

"Oh yea. I remember you. Meet me at the same spot."

"Cool I just need twenty minutes."

"Hit me when you are there. I'll be around." Following the call, I texted Emily, "I'll be a little bit later than expected. Riley should be back shortly."

"No problem. We're all good over here," she replied.

When I got to Mission Beach, I scoped out the area to make sure it was safe to get out. I went to the spot and did not see J-Money, so I called him. He said, "I'll be there in a minute. I had to make a run." I waited there for about five minutes until he finally came. When he did, he brought someone else with him.

"Who's he?"

"Just a friend. Don't worry about him." How many do you want?" I had done my research on the street value, so I was looking for a bundle at wholesale price.

"Five hundred pills."

"Damn you really like to party. I do not have that kind of work on me, but do you have the money on you."

"No, it's nearby. I have someone holding it. Can you get a hold of that much?"

"Yea I know someone who can take care of you. Hold on. I have to make a call." He walked off and was talking on the phone. He came back moments later.

"You and your friend can follow us."

When we were on the road, I noticed we circled a few blocks repeatedly. I guess they were trying to make sure I was not being tailed. When we got to our destination it was not what I expected. We were in the suburbs of North Claremont. We pulled in a driveway

114

and into the garage. I got out of the car and J-Money said, "Where's your friend?"

"I don't have a friend. It is nothing personal. I wasn't sure if I could trust you." He laughed.

"You couldn't. Well played."

That is when a middle-aged white man came out of the house. He had a tapered fade, wore glasses, a plaid shirt, jeans, and beat up sneakers. He looked like he designed computer software in Silicon Valley. He was not at all what I expected but then again, I am not your typical drug dealer either.

He was cocky and had a dorky disingenuous smile on his face. The first thing he said was, "Hey J. Who's our new friend?"

"This is P," J-Money replied. Then the guy turned his attention to me.

"What's P stand for, friend?"

"Pierce." While sticking his hand out for a handshake he said, "Hey Pierce. I am Craig. I hear you're looking for something I could possibly help with." I reciprocate the gesture.

"I need five hundred pills." He whistled.

"That's a lot of pills. What do you plan to do with them?"

"What does it matter? I am looking for a supplier. I was hoping we could go into business together."

"Are you a cop Pierce?"

"Do I look like a cop?"

"I don't know do you?" He then grabbed a security wand and patted me down.

"I'm clean. Can we do business now?"

"That's still to be determined. I have never seen you before. Where are you from?"

"I've never seen you before either." He chuckled.

"I see you have a sense of humor. The thing is though. I don't find anything funny." Things were starting to get intense, so I dialed it down.

"Look I don't mean any disrespect. I'm a local guy looking for a supplier I can count on and make a lot of money with." He started laughing.

"Relax. I am just fucking with you. How much do you have?"

"I have five thousand dollars." That was the last of my personal savings.

"Well that's a problem because what you're asking for is eight thousand dollars."

"That's not my understanding for how much five hundred pills is."

"Well friend. I do not know who told you that but that is the price. Take it or leave it." I did not have a choice. I had no other options. Plus, I knew I would make my money back. "I'll give you five thousand now and write you a check for the remaining three thousand dollars." He laughed.

"Do I look like a bank? This is what we are going to do. I'll take the five thousand dollars now and you'll pay me back the other three thousand dollars with interest." I was beginning to not like this guy more and more, but I took it. I gave him the money.

"I'm going to need to see your driver's license too?"

"For what?"

"To protect my interest." As he held his hand out, I hesitated to hand it over. After all this was now compromising my family's safety. However, I was already in this situation and I had to follow through with it, so I handed it over. He took the license and photocopied it. Then he walked it back over to me with a smug look on his face and said, "Here you go. You can follow J-Money to get the product."

We went to another location to get the drugs and the next thing I know I was transporting drugs across town in my own truck. It was even more nerve wracking than driving the work truck across the border, but I made it home safely. I walked into the condo and it was quiet. I figured everyone was asleep. I went into the den and started placing the five hundred pills in individuals' baggies to be sold at thirty dollars apiece. I would make fifteen thousand off of the first batch. Even though I had to pay Craig back with interest I would still make a profit. As I was finishing up, I felt a hand touch my shoulder and a voice say to me, "What are you doing?!" I turned around in the chair and it was Riley. When we made eye contact my eyes opened wide and my jaw dropped.

"It's not what it looks like."

"Why do you have all those pills?!" I was speechless and did not know what to say so I remained silent.

"You need to start talking because from where I'm standing it looks like you're sneaking around and bagging up pills in our home to sell."

"It's not like that. I just didn't expect anybody to be up."

"I bet you didn't but that doesn't explain anything. Why are you doing this Pierce?!"

"I'm holding it for someone."

"So, you put our families lives at risk to cover up for someone else?" My plan was falling apart before it even started. I was caught and knew I had to be straight with her.

"No. Can you lower your voice, so we don't wake Junior up." I took both of my hands and rubbed my face. "Your right I'm selling pills but it's really not that big of a deal."

"Are you serious Pierce. Not that big of a deal. This could not only get you in trouble but me as well. You brought the drugs into our home. What are you thinking?"

"I'm thinking about us. I want to contribute, and this is how I do that."

"We don't need anything. I'm taking care of us."

"Do you hear yourself. Yea you are taking care of us and that is the problem. I am the one who should be doing that."

"And you think this is the answer?"

"I don't know but it's the best opportunity I have. I need this Riley. You have to let me do this."

"You expect me to support you being a drug dealer?"

"I don't expect anything. Especially not support from you because when have I ever gotten that?"

"You ungrateful fuck. I have done nothing but support you. I have sat here and watched you tear yourself apart for years while neglecting my own needs. If you haven't noticed I am the only one here for you when you need them so save that bullshit for someone else because I am not the one!" I stood up out of the chair, walked to the corner of the room, and looked out the window.

"I am sorry. You are right Riley. I should not have bought the drugs here and it will not happen again. I have directed my anger at the wrong person for years. You are not my enemy. You are actually the best person

118

I have ever had in my life. I could not have asked for a better wife. You may not know it, but you motivate me every day to be a better man and I will be. I know this makes no sense to you but do not stop believing in me now. I would not do this if I felt my family was in danger. I have a plan. Just hear me out." I told her my plan and explained all the details. She actually thought the strip club was a good idea. However, she did not throw caution to the wind. She still had her doubts but wanted to support me. She walked over to me and grabbed my hands.

"Something tells me I couldn't convince you otherwise if I wanted to." I smirked.

"Probably not." She let my hands go. and sat in the chair.

"My whole life my father tried to keep me away from men like himself and I'm married to a man just like him."

"What do you mean?"

"I always act like I don't know what my father does for a living, but I do. I just choose to ignore it."

"What does he do?" She smiled and looked me dead in the eyes.

"He's a drug dealer Pierce." She looked away and paused for a moment. Then continued to say, "And I'm no better because now I'm helping him infiltrate the pharmaceutical business."

"So, is that the business you were attending to on our vacation?"

"Yea."

"Well, it doesn't make you a bad person because you're helping him. If anything, it shows how great of a person you are. Family is what we have, and we must stick together."

"Yea, I suppose so." Then she said, "Your plan is not bad, but we need to minimize the risk more if I'm going to support you."

"What do you propose?"

"The less people who know the better. Where are you getting the pills?"

"Some guy named Craig in North Claremont."

"How long have you been dealing with him?"

This is the first time."

"Good. End it."

"Then where will I get the pills?"

"You did hear me say my dad is a drug dealer right."

"I can't buy drugs from your dad."

"But you can get them from some random guy named Craig?"

"Fair point but I don't want your dad knowing I sell drugs."

"Don't worry he won't. He won't even know I am involved. Just let me take care of it."

"Okay."

"Who else knows about this?"

"Only Mikey?"

"Let us keep it that way. We can talk about the rest of this later. Let's go to bed."

When that day started, I did not imagine Riley would find out about my plans of selling drugs. She would be risking everything for me. I definitely did not think she would be on board with helping. However, she was, and I could not have been more thrilled. I stashed the pills away and laid in bed next to her. I learned more about her in that moment then I did in the course of our relationship. I rolled over and kissed her on the forehead goodnight. Then I turned onto my back and looked up at the ceiling fan. I thought to myself, "Welcome to the Drug game."

Chapter XIIII

Summer '16 (Pierce)

The past two years have been good to me. Many things had changed in my life and I liked to think for the better. I started working part time at my job and now have a successful business. I ended up naming the club "CandyLand." It had been open for two years and there was not a sweet tooth we could not fix with our product. I was able to turn an idea into reality. I was the owner but like me and Riley discussed it was best to operate in the background. I let Mikey be the face of the business. He also handled our security. The traffic we were getting in the club was mind blowing. It turns out pussy and pills are the perfect combination.

I also brought on the kid who sold me my first pill J-Money. I did not know he was only sixteen years old at the time because he looked like a grown man. He had facial hair and all. Nonetheless it was good having him around. He was young, energetic, and full of life. We needed that type of energy around us. It kept us in tune with the new generation. He had been real with me and had a lot of potential, so I asked him to join our team. To my surprise he was an aspiring artist and had a local hit out called, "Trenches." It was buzzing throughout the city and was viral on the internet. I actually saw some of me in him.

Despite our unfavorable starts in life we still wanted better for ourselves. Unlike his last employer I wanted to help him get out of the drug game and live his dream. He did not sell drugs for me, but I would let him perform in the club as the headlining act from time to time to make some money legitimately. He was also doing shows all over California. Unfortunately, he loved the streets too much and would get in trouble every now and then. It was like quicksand and he was sinking in it. He could not stay away. It was all he knew. I figured I would look out for him and let him come to his own realization of what he wanted to do with his life. I just hoped he figured it out before it was too late.

As far as Craig goes, I dealt with him only that one time. I ended up paying him the three thousand with the interest plus extra for the photocopy of my license. Now I was getting my supply from my wife. I did not have to deal with a middleman. I was able to trickle the benefits down to the customers by having cheaper prices then the competition. My customers loved it and often told me it was to die for.

The past three months we had sold around three hundred and fifty thousand pills priced at ten dollars each. That was enough to serve a quarter of the city's population. My operation had gotten up to making around 1.16 million dollars a month in revenue. I did not know what to do with all of the money, but we found ways to use it. I was a reasonable and generous man who liked to spread the wealth. I looked out for my people. I did what was needed to earn their loyalty and respect. It was not many of us in our operation, but we were strong, and we were doing it all with no violence. Luckily, we had not been put in the position to go against that ideal.

Even with all the success there came a different type of stress, but I still had Dr. Shaw to help keep my mind at ease. She had been happy with my continuous progress and so was I. She always reminded me how rare it is for someone to make a complete turnaround in their life the way I did. I was proud of how far I came but I was not satisfied. I could still do more. The success of my organization was proof.

I had no idea where I wanted to go from there. I had not thought that far ahead. It seemed like the less I thought the better off I was. If I actually took the time to think deeply about what I was doing, I would still only be a truck driver. However, the cons outweigh the pros for your average person but that was just it. I was tired of being average. I wanted to stand out. I had to be seen as more than an average guy. I refused for that to be the narrative of my life. I believed the world was mine and I went after it.

The hardest part of my success was having to be two different people. Since I did not want to attract any unwanted attention and Riley preferred, I was low key about my newfound fortune. I had to be more subtle at home and act like nothing had changed. However, when I was at the club it was the complete opposite. I wore designers' clothes and jewelry. I always had stacks of money handy to buy whatever I may want. I drove around in one of many luxury cars I kept in a garage I rented. Along with many other outlandish things I would do from time to time. I was definitely feeling myself.

The thing that was different about this day was I learned my success had attracted the attention of others.

As I was getting in my car after leaving the club I was ambushed, beat up, blind folded, and my hands were zipped tied behind my back. They threw me in the trunk and drove off. I was completely blindsided by this. I had no enemies at least that I was aware of. Thoughts of who it could be and what was going to happen to me ran through my mind.

I thought it was all over for me. My whole life flashed before my eyes. It felt like my luck had finally run out and now it was time to pay the ultimate price. I had run that scenario through my mind so many times. I just never thought it would actually happen. At that moment I became a praying man. I promised that if I had gotten out of that situation I would change.

The ride was dreadful and seemed like forever. It must have been the hottest day of the summer. I felt like I was melting. The trunk was dingy and smelt like gas. There was something hard underneath me digging in my side and I could not adjust my body to get more comfortable. It also felt like they were hitting every bump in the road. I must have hit my head a dozen times and just to think that was only the beginning.

Suddenly the car stopped. I could hear the men talking amongst themselves, but their voices were hard to hear. I did not understand what was going on. I had been flying under the radar for so long. What changed? However, I was about to find out why I was summoned. When they opened the trunk there were three guns pointed at me. They pulled me out the trunk, took me to a room, unrestrained my arms, sat me on a chair, and took off the blindfold. When I opened my eyes, I was surprised to see Nina sitting across the table from me with a man named Dame and two other men I had not seen before.

The first thing she said was, "Do you know who I am?" I did not respond. I remained quiet knowing that nothing I said would make the situation better. She continued to say, "Of course you do. You have been in my restaurant multiple times. Still no words for me Pierce." I could not believe she knew who I was. I knew nothing good was going to come from this conversation for me. I remained quiet. I did not want to get on her bad side, not that I was not already.

Then she said, "I've been watching you Pierce and it turns out that you're the reason I've been losing business and I can't have that. You are pissing off a lot of people and becoming a problem. What do you think I should do about it?" I knew if I was going to speak this was the time. I did not want to leave it completely up to her to choose my fate. I looked at her and the other guys in the room. I could see it in their eyes that I had fucked up. She grabbed my face and said, "You better say something before I lose what little patients I have." Like many times before I felt hopeless. I was not ready to have it all end there. I still had something to live for.

"How can I make it right?" She smirked at me.

"So, he can speak. For starters, who do you work for?"

"I work alone." She laughed and then smacked me.

"You think this is a joke. You better speak now or forever hold your peace."

"Okay," I muttered.

"You have something to say?"

"Yes."

"Explain to me how a guy like you can get your hands on that much product. Who is your supplier?" I was not stupid. The only reason she would keep me alive is because I posed no threat to her life and had information that she wanted. I just had to keep it that way. However, I needed to give her something good to calm her down. After all my life depended on it. I took a gulp.

"It's a guy from China." From her facial expression I could tell she had enough. She looked over at Dame and nodded her head.

He walked over toward me and began to beat on me. The first punch was on the side of my head which dazed me. From then on there was a flurry of punches I could barely see. It lasted for a few minutes but felt like an eternity. I vividly remember spitting out one of my teeth. Even though my life laid in the balance the only thing I thought of in that moment was thank goodness it was a molar. I did not know how I would be able to explain one of my front teeth being knocked out if I made it out of their home.

When he stopped hitting me Nina held me by my hair to keep my head from slumping over. She asked me the same question and I repeated the same thing. I could not tell her everything because that would involve bringing my family into this and she would not need me anymore. "Okay. I guess there's nothing to tell," she exclaimed. Momentarily I saw a glimmer of hope. Until she said, "So that means I have no use for you." She pulled her gun from her waistline, cocked it, and pointed it between my eyes. Though I was out of it. I could consciously here her utter the words, "I'll send your regards to that pretty lawyer wife of yours." I felt my heart drop in my stomach. I had to choose between the lesser of the two evils. There was no way I would let my wife pay for my sins.

My lips were swollen, and my jaw was stiff. I could barely talk. I tried to say something but found it difficult to speak. She poked me with her gun. "What was that?"

"I'll give you my supplier. Just leave my family out of it," I mumbled.

"I'm listening."

"His name is Ray." Ray was the one actually getting the drugs and bringing them to me for Riley. She looked at me unconvinced.

"I've never heard of this Ray. Tell me more."

I gave her some minor details about him while nodding in and out of consciousness. I hoped it was enough to get me out of there but of course she wanted more from me first. She had me call him on speakerphone and set up a meeting on the spot. I pulled out my phone, went into my contacts, and called. I had no idea where this conversation was going to go, and I did not want any extra information slipping out. When he answered I said, "Hey Ray."

"Hey Pierce. What's up?"

"I need to meet with you about expanding our business."

"Okay. Is our current situation not working out?"

"Yea it's all good. I just ran into another opportunity that could benefit us both. I just want to introduce you to someone and run it by you."

"Okay did you run this by R." I cut him off before he could say Riley's name.

"No need. This is something for us."

"I'll be back in the states in a couple of days. I'll call you when I'm around."

After the call Nina said, "You better pray this guy is

who you say he is. If not, our next meeting will have a different ending."

"I told you everything." She gave Dame a phone then turned her attention back to me.

"You better hope so because you and your family's lives depend on it. Call me on this phone when he calls you and I'll tell you where we're meeting at." On her way out she stopped in front of Dame and one of the other guys. "Clean this mess up. Then get him out of here."

Dame looked at me with despair. He threw a rag and bottle of water at me. "Clean yourself up." I poured water on the rag and wiped my face. The rag was drenched in blood almost instantly.

I asked, "Can I have another rag?"

"You have one. Make it work and hurry up we have to go." I used every clean corner of the rag until it was completely red. He blindfolded me again then forcibly grabbed me by my arm. He stood me up and tied my arms. "Let's go."

He left the other guy behind to clean everything up. We walked for a moment and then stopped. When I heard the trunk pop open. I said, "There's no need for me to ride in the trunk again.

"Shut up and get in."

"If you're going to make me ride in there can you at least remove whatever that is I had to lay on?" He did not respond but I heard him move something then he forcibly pushed me inside. There was a moment of silence before he shut the trunk door.

"Shut your ass up." Then threw whatever it was he took out on top of me.

While we were riding, I kept thinking something

would happen that would change her mind and I would not get out of there in one piece. As I laid still in the trunk my body felt like I had been hit by a car. It was throbbing nonstop with pain. At that moment I realized everything I built was just a façade. I did not have the faintest idea of what to do next. The car stopped and I froze still awaiting what was to come next.

   He pulled me out the trunk and cut the zip tie. He put a phone in my hand and said, "Call the number inside this phone when it's time. See you soon." Then I heard him walking away followed by a door closing and tires peeling off. I quickly ripped off the blindfold. I still could not see clearly since one of my eyes was too swollen and I kept squinting the other one due to the sensitivity from the light.

   I immediately patted my body to see if I was still all together. I could not believe I was still alive. When my vision cleared up a bit. I looked around and noticed I was in the CandyLand parking lot. I pulled myself together and walked up to the building. After I unlocked the back door and went to open it. I collapsed falling through the doorway.

Chapter XV

Empire (Nina)

We have established ourselves from San Diego to LA but the past couple of months have been tough. Recently I ran into trouble with the cartel because of their inability to keep up with supply due to a gang war with their rival. I started to venture off and use other suppliers to keep up with my demand and that did not sit well with them. Now we are at odds. A few months ago, my operation was moving a hundred keys of china white in San Diego alone which was making me 4.5 million dollars a month in profit and I was moving double that in LA. I was racking in about 13.5 million dollars a month just off heroin.

More recently my profits have started to fall, and it came to my attention that a man named Pierce was responsible for it. He had been making a hard push into my market with his pills. For some reason, the addicts thought it made it better if they were popping a pill versus shooting up. He was stealing some of my clients by selling that shit. It seemed he wanted some attention and now he got it. Lately I've been keeping the peace on the streets but now I have to remind everyone why I'm the wrong bitch to be fucking with.

Following my conversation with Pierce I had another meeting with Mayor Wallace and Police Chief

McDonald set up at a nearby outlet mall. We were meeting at a soul food spot in Valencia Park. Today I had to make my monthly payment of fifty thousand dollars apiece for the protection of me and my product. Now I needed their help with some street shit. As they ate lunch, I filled them in on my problem. As usual McDonald was an arrogant prick. The first thing he said was, "I knew you would eventually need our help with the competition."

"I don't need shit. It is in both of our interest to get rid of them. Do not forget I pay you. But there are two other options: I could lose business and we both make less, or I could deal with it myself and kill everybody. Which option do you prefer?" He did not respond. He just brushed it off because he knew I was right. We were all in this together. My loss was there is too.

"There's no need to argue amongst each other. We just need to come up with a solution that will benefit us both. How can we help you," asked Mayor Wallace?

"I found out who's been stealing business from me. His name is Pierce. I believe you're familiar with him, Mayor."

"No, I don't believe so."

"No, I believe you do. You were talking to him and his wife a while back at my restaurant."

"I'm not sure what or who you're referring to."

"Okay, let me refresh your memory. His wife is a beautiful Asian big-time lawyer in this city."

"You're not referring to Riley, are you?" I snapped my fingers.

"That's her name. Yes, I'm referring to Riley."

"No way. Her husband is just a regular guy who drives trucks for living. He's actually one of the drivers for our shipments from Mexico."

"Yea. Well it appears he's double dipping."

"Wow. I don't believe it."

"Well believe it. He is making a killing out of a strip club called CandyLand and right now I am working on establishing a relationship with his supplier. Once I get it all sorted out. You can bust him. That way you get your collar and I get rid of the competition. It's a win-win for both of us."

"Why don't we just get it over with tonight," asked McDonald?

"It's not that simple. The supplier is coming in from out of the country so it's going to take some time to set it up."

"Okay let us know when everything is ready," said Wallace. I stood up out of my seat.

"So, I guess we're all good here fellas."

McDonald glared at me while Wallace said, "Yea we're good. Right McDonald?"

"Yea. Sure."

"Good." There was nothing else to talk about so I gave them the envelope of cash and before I left, I said, "I'm sure you can afford to pick up the tab for my drink. Talk soon." When I walked outside Jason had already had the car door open for me. When he got inside, he turned around.

"Where to now?"

"The Den I have to meet back up with Dame." After the ride back to the club I stopped Jason from parking.

"Don't get out of the car. I want you to go up to LA and make sure everything is running smoothly while we deal with everything down here."

"Sure thing." I walked into my office and Dame was

sitting in my chair.

I asked, "You okay?"

"Yea. I am good. Why?"

"Because you're sitting in my seat. You must have bumped your head or something." We laughed.

"Oh, my bad. You want me to get up?"

"Nah you're good. How'd the drop off go?"

"It was cool. He's still alive."

"Do you think he's bullshitting us?"

"I'm not sure but I do know we scared the shit out of him because he smelled like piss." We laughed. Then he said, "But all jokes aside. We will see when he sets up the meeting. Speaking of meetings. How did yours go with Wallace and McDonald?"

"Other than having to look at punk ass McDonald's ugly face it was alright. I told them about our new friend. They're going to take care of him for us after we get our new supplier."

"Don't let him get to you. Let's just focus on stacking this money."

"For sure. I want you to stay down here until we deal with this issue."

"Awe you miss me huh?" I smiled.

"Don't flatter yourself. I just want my best man around until this is all cleared up."

"What about LA?"

"I already sent Jason to hold it down up there."

"Damn. What if I did not want to stay," he replied jokingly.

"That's not an option."

"Okay boss lady. What's the move tonight?"

"Nothing planned. What would you like to do?"

"Honestly, we can just chill and call some bitches

up?"

"Sounds good to me. I will set it up but first we got to stop by and see my mama. She's been asking about you too."

"No doubt."

Before we left, I sent a text out to one of my main girls, Brittany and told her to bring a friend with her to the penthouse tonight. My mom lived in Emerald Hills. I loved going back home but hated it at the same time. I had some good times there but just as many bad. It is a part of me, but I have moved on. I would not be going back now if my mom would leave. It is all good though I am thankful she is still around so I can see her. On the way to her house me and Dame were cruising with our seats back puffing a blunt. The music was bumping, and it felt good just like old times.

When we pulled up there was a group of people standing in front of the house. When we got closer, I could hear arguing. Dame said, "You know them

"Not sure. Grab your gun." I got out of the car and tucked the gun in my waistline. I approached the crowd and saw my brother cursing at another man. I hoped in between them.

"Yo, Are we good?"

"No, we are not. This fool needs to stop disrespecting my sister and take care of his child," replied the man.

"Man get the fuck out of here. You need to worry about your own kids. I got mine," my brother replied.

"You ain't got shit. I should beat your ass." I looked in the doorway and saw my mom. I needed to stop them, so I interjected.

"Look my man, you need to take a hike and cool

off."

"Make me." Dame branded his gun.

"She isn't asking." The guy froze up.

"Okay, y'all got that. I'll get with him another time." We diffused the situation and the crowd broke up. I stood there as he walked away to make sure there was not going to be any more problems.

When they cleared out, I turned to my brother and said, "Damn Drew. You just got out and already starting shit." He laughed and gave me a hug.

"I missed you too." He turned to dame and greeted him.

"How you bro?"

"I'm good. The question is, how are you?"

"I'm good. That shit there was not about nothing. It is always something with that girl, but I see you two are still thick as thieves. Rich thieves from what I hear."

"What did you hear," I asked?

"Come on. You know it is always somebody coming into prison with stories from the streets and you two are buzzing in there. I need to get put on."

"Forget about all that. It has been a minute since you have been out in the free world. I'm just happy to see you."

That is when mom said, "Y'all get in here and get something to eat."

"Yes mam! You don't have to ask me twice," Dame replied. He loved her cooking. We all did. We gathered around the table while we talked and ate. We reminisced about stories from the past and rejoiced in the present. It was moments like this that I enjoyed. There is not any amount of money that can replace this feeling.

After we left that is when the party started. I had

already received a text from Brittany saying that
Will(doorman) let them up to the penthouse. When we
got to my place, they both were already tipsy. As soon as
I came through the door, she ran up to me and jumped
into my arms. "I missed you!"
"Clearly. How much did you drink?"
"Only three shots of cognac. Right Kait."
"You might want to slow down a little. You're
already wilding out."
"Your wilding out. I am good. Let's all get in the hot
tub." Dame did not hesitate.
"I'm down." I told them to get in and I would join
them in a minute. I had to do one more thing before I
indulged. I still had the duffel bag of money Dame
dropped earlier out in the open. I went into my bedroom
and shut the door behind me. I stashed the cash in my
safe that was hidden in my closet. Afterwards I took a
brief moment to be alone to collect myself. While I was
sitting there my phone started ringing.
    Just as I thought things couldn't get any worse. I got
a call from one of my people in LA. They had just raided
one of my buildings and arrested Jason. I hurried up and
turned on the news. The reporter Wendy Summers was
all over it. She claims she lost a lot of friends to the
violence from the drug trade. She had a personal
vendetta against everybody she thought was involved.
This bust was not good at all. I had to get Jason out
ASAP and separate myself from this. Wendy was
already trying to link this to me by calling me the
mastermind to the drug epidemic that plagued
California.
    This was a major setback. It was like the harder I
worked to get out. Life worked that much harder to pull

me back down. Nevertheless, this is not the life for the weak hearted. Nothing about it is simple. For now, I need to figure out my next move. First thing first I need to tell Dame and get some more information to see what is going on. I walked out to the hot tub and said to our guest, "You two bitches got to go." They just looked at me like I was joking. I turned off the music. "I'm serious like right now get your shit and go!" They finally got the memo and started getting out of the tub.

As they walked past me Brittany said, "Whatever. You are on some bullshit. I don't even know why I fuck with you."

I could see Dame was annoyed but I knew in a moment he would understand what was going on.

"What just crawled up your ass."

"Our asses just got handed to us in LA. They raided the spot and got Jason."

"Stop playing. I already took care of the city officials up there."

"Well maybe not well enough because they just busted up our shit."

"Don't do that. It is the same set up we have down here, and they were all on board with it."

"I don't know what's going on but let us get out of here and find out. Somebody knows something." He got dressed, I grabbed the keys, and we hit the streets.

Chapter XVI

In Too Deep (Pierce)

I woke up with my back leaned against the wall and a glass of water being tossed in my face. I could not remember what had happened. With my swollen lips I mumbled, "Where am I?"

"At the club. In your office. What happened bro," asked Mikey?

"You don't want to know."

"Try me?"

"Help me sit up and somebody grab me a drink with ibuprofen. I feel like shit."

"You look like shit." He sat me on the couch and Natalie got me the drink and pills. She also brought me a bag of ice and held it to my face as I leaned my head back.

"What's going on Pierce," asked Natalie?

" Yea what's up? Talk to us," added Mikey.

"We fucked up. Nina knows about us. After I left earlier, they kidnapped me and fucked me up."

"What did they want," Mikey asked frantically.

"They wanted to know who's our supplier."

"What did you tell them?"

"I told them what they wanted to hear."

"Fuck. There trying to take us out. You can't introduce them to your supplier."

"I have too. She threatened to kill my wife." He grabbed his face with both hands.

"This situation is fucked either way look at it."

"I know but we'll figure something out."

"You better because our lives depend on it."

"Calm down. Give me some time to get myself together and we'll talk in a little bit." He stormed out of the office out uneasy.

I fell asleep shortly after that conversation and woke up around 3 o'clock in the morning. When I awoke Natalie was still there sitting up on the couch sleeping with my head on her lap. I felt safe there and did not want to get up, so I laid there a while longer. I checked my phone and saw a few missed calls and text messages from Riley. I knew I would not hear the end of this when I got home. I turned my head to Natalie and called her name softly. She opened her eyes slowly and smiled.

"Hey there. You're up," she said.

"Thanks for staying with me."

"I had to. You were in pretty bad shape."

"Are we the only ones here?

"No Mikey had a few guys stay here for security."

"Good."

"Do you feel any better?"

"Yea, a lot better thanks to you." I got up and looked in the mirror. Then I said, "The swelling went down some too. I'll be ready in no time to get back to my modeling career." We laughed

"Well the bruises actually look good on you." I blushed.

"You're just being nice, but I appreciate it."

I made some coffee and poured us both a cup. I gave her the cup and she said, "Thanks."

I sat next to her and said jokingly, "Since I'll probably get killed soon. I want you to know it has been a pleasure working with you. You're actually pretty amazing now that I've gotten the chance to know you." She smiled from ear to ear.

"You're going to make it through this. Do not start saying goodbyes yet. Thanks for the compliment but what did you think of me before?"

"Honestly?"

"I expect nothing but the truth." I thought about it for a moment before I responded.

"The first time I saw you. I thought it had to be a joke when you asked me to drink with you. A girl like you could have anybody. Since that night I wondered if I made a mistake not being with you. Then when I saw you again in the club you were the only person I could see in the room. I mean there were other people around, but I was completely captivated by your presents. Nothing else mattered. Then when I found out it was you it felt like a second chance. Even though you were a little uninviting."

"I'm sorry I didn't mean anything by it."

"It's fine. I know you did not. You probably hear stuff like this all the time." She laughed.

"No, usually it's more like hey sexy, hey baby." We both laughed.

"Since I'm being honest. I still feel that way around you now."

At that moment there was chemistry between us. A feeling I had not felt in a long time. We locked eyes, inched closer to each other, and began to lean in for a kiss when we were interrupted by someone banging on the door. In complete aggravation I leaned my head back, looked at the ceiling, and thought to myself, "Why?" I opened the door and it was Tony. He was one of our armed security guards. He said, "There's a man out here saying he's Natalie's boyfriend."

"Oh Shit! It's Casey and he's not my boyfriend anymore," she replied.

"I can tell him to scram."

"Is this the friends whose house we were at when we met," I asked.

"Yup."

"Well, let's go talk to him. I've always been interested in knowing what your type was." We got ourselves together then walked out to the main entrance where he was at.

He was a pretty basic guy. Not what I expected but, in his defense, he was intoxicated. He had on a gray suit, a white dress shirt that was unbuttoned halfway down, and a loose tie. I said, "Can I help you sir?"

"My name is Casey."

"What can I do for you Casey? We're closed right now."

"Is Natalie here?" Natalie was standing in the distance in the corner of the room.

"Would you like to speak to him?"

"No, I rather not."

"Come on Natalie let's go home!"

"No, I told you it's over."

"You say that all the time, but we always get back together. I am sorry. Can we go now?"

"I mean it this time. Just leave me alone Casey."

"I said. Let's go!"

"I think it's time for you to go and sober up some buddy," I said.

"I'm not your buddy. Who the fuck are you anyway? Her new boyfriend."

I reiterated, "I'm going to tell you nicely again. It's time to go."

When I went to go direct him off my property. He pushed past me and ran after Natalie and grabbed her. She resisted so he slapped her. Me and Tony ran over after him. When he went to raise his hand again. I pistol whipped him and pointed my gun at the back of his head. At that point I had not ever pulled a gun on anyone. I did not even carry one on me usually but after what happened yesterday. I felt obligated to carry protection. He stopped and I said, "If you hit her again. I'll blow your fucking head off." He raised his arms in the air.

"Okay man. I'm leaving." He got up and walked toward the door holding the back of his head.

"You'll regret this but then it'll be too late." I shut the door behind him and locked it. I helped her up and sat her in a chair at the bar. I grabbed her some ice, sat next to her, and began icing her cheek.

"Are you okay?"

"Yea I'm fine. He has been taking the breakup hard this time. Casey is actually really a nice guy, he's just mad."

"I'm sorry you don't deserve that." She hugged me and said nothing else.

Chapter XVII

Amends (Riley)

I was awakened from the sound of Pierce coming inside the house early in the morning. Yesterday I did not see or hear from him all day. I was not happy. There was no way I was going to let him make me look like a fool. I got up and went downstairs to address him. When I got downstairs, I was shocked to find out his face was bruised and battered. "What happened?" He moved away as I went to touch his face.

"I had an accident." I knew it was more to the story. A blind man could see he was lying.

"What kind of accident? Where?"

"I was hanging out with the guys and we got into a little fight."

"That doesn't look like a little fight and what are you doing fighting?" He walked away as I was talking.

"It's not a big deal." I was beginning to lose all symphony for him, but I was not going to push him. I walked in the master bathroom after him.

"You couldn't call or have someone else let me know what was going on?"

"Really Riley. You were the last thing I was thinking about." He was being a jerk. I tried to keep it civilized so I ignored his last statement.

"Where did you end up staying?"

"At Mikey's."

"So, you road out of the city further away. Instead of coming home."

"What am I on trial? I'm not in the mood for this." His story did not add up. The truth would come to light soon or later. He pretty much avoided me from that point on until he left. He even said bye to Junior and walked by me as if I was not there. He could be such a baby. I got Junior ready for school so I could focus on the task I have to complete today. Specifically, the affairs dealing with dads' business. Speaking of dad, he was calling me.

He called because he wanted me and Kate to go to China and meet with new potential partners. Shortly after speaking with dad Martin called. He stressed to me the matter was urgent and he wanted to meet immediately. After I dropped Junior off at school. I hurried to the firm. When I entered his office, he looked worried. He was even a little hesitant to tell me what was going on. "What's wrong?" He stopped biting his nails and rubbed his hands together.

"We have a problem."

"And what would that be?" I was now becoming frustrated with all the suspense. I had no idea of what he was talking about.

"The California courts have requested Smith & Walton to provide their secret files." After years of fighting this from happening it finally did despite our best efforts.

"Fuck. This is a problem."

"Yes. I know."

"What's your plan?"

"That's why I called you so we could come up with

one. I'm sure you thought of the possibility that this would happen." Truth is I have not thought much about it lately. I felt like our team had this case under control. On top of that I had been so occupied with building the family business and dealing with Pierce that the firm had taken a backseat. Nonetheless my reputation was based on the success of the firm. I had to come up with something.

"Once those documents get released it'll be hard to say their intentions were pure per se. It is going to leave us vulnerable. At this point our defeat is inevitable. We need to minimize the damage as much as possible. I recommend we file for Chapter 11 Bankruptcy. That way we can freeze the litigation and once it's moved to bankruptcy court, we can negotiate our settlements."

"I agree. This is our best option but how do we convince Jason?"

"I'm not sure if we need to set up an appointment with him."

"No need. You know him. He is already on his way here. He'll be here in like thirty minutes give or take."

"Okay. I'll meet you in the boardroom in ten minutes."

I walked into my office, grabbed a bottle of water, and took a deep breath. I reminded myself that I was the one who wanted to be big time. These are the situations that you endure and must overcome on the journey to the top. I took a few minutes to make a call to Kate and verify that everything was set for our trip later. After that I headed to the board room. Martin was the only one there Jason had not arrived yet.

He said, "It never gets easier. I survived all these years telling myself it would but you Riley are made for this. One of the best if not the best lawyer I've ever seen, and you'll continue to do great things."

"Why are you saying this?"

"After this case I'll be retiring, and I will be recommending you to be a senior partner." I was shocked and did not know what to say. I was flattered by his kind words but knew I would miss him.

I gathered myself and replied, "Thank you. I really appreciate that, but I'll save my goodbyes for after the case." Moments later Jason stormed through the boardroom doors frantically.

"Have you heard the great news dream team?"

"Hello to you too."

"I thought your firm had this under control."

"We lost the battle not the war so let's deal with the issues in front of us."

"There is no us. I am the one getting sued. I'm not even sure if you all are the right fit for my company anymore."

"I fear that if you leave us now, you'd be making a big mistake. Have you discussed this with the other board members," asked Martin?

"Why would I? I am the chairman. I make the decisions and know what's best."

"That may be so but what I think Martin is saying is there is no other firm who could have held off the request for those documents like we did for years. Even with that huge blow we have another suggestion on how to soften the blow if you'd like to hear it?" Martin looked over at me with no expression on his face. Meanwhile Jason was walking around the room pondering thoughts that I could not imagine. I just hoped I did enough to salvage our relationship with him. Eventually, he came to a stop and looked at us both. Before saying anything, he twirled his wedding ring around his finger a few times.

Then he stopped and said, "Okay let's hear this new plan of yours."

"Certainly," Martin replied. Then he asked everyone to take a seat so I could explain it.

After my brief presentation Jason asked, "What will happen to the business after this?"

"It will survive and maintain its value."

"And will I have to give up any of my own personal money?"

"More than likely at some point you will have to reach a settlement for lawsuits against you, but it will be nowhere near what they're asking for now. Plus, this will protect you from future financial liability. There is one thing though."

"And that is?"

"It may come to a point where it will be in the companies and your best interest if you give up control of it."

"I will admit I like everything you said to me today other than giving up control of the company my grandfather built. I hope you find an alternative solution because that will never happen."

"I assure you that I will continue to do my best and give you the best possible representation."

"Make sure you do." He shook me and Martin's hands then exited the room.

When he left Martin walked up to me. "Good work Riley. You just saved our butts. It would be a bad look if one of our biggest clients dumped us in the middle of a case."

"It would be. I need you to do me a favor."
"Favor?"
"Can you handle this until I come back? I'll only be out of town for a couple days."
"Is everything okay?"
"I just have some family issues I need to address."
"Is there anything I can do?"
While smiling I replied, "Yes there is. Cover for me." He laughed.
"Right. After all you have done for this firm. It won't be a problem."
"You sure you're going to be okay?"
"Yea. We already got the ball rolling. I'll be good."
"Thanks Martin. You're the best."
I went to my office and cleared my schedule for the next couple days. Then I grabbed anything I would need while I was away. Our flight was scheduled for tomorrow afternoon so we would get to China in the morning. I just had to prepare a few things at home. After that for the remainder of the day I will spend the rest of the time playing my favorite role of mommy to my baby boy. Tomorrow I will focus on the task ahead. Things would work out at the end. However, I cannot believe how far I have come two years after me and dad's meeting on the balcony in Hong Kong, and me and Pierce's conversation in the den. Somehow things have worked out. Nonetheless, as much as I enjoy it sometimes, I think of the days when life was much simpler, but I understand those days are gone so the current situation will have to do.

Chapter XVIII

Stay Afloat (Pierce)

My back may have been against the wall, but it was not the first time. Riley had just gone out of town for business and I could not get Natalie off my mind. I had already called Emily to see if Junior could stay with her for a few days while I worked on getting things back in order. After I dropped Junior off, I went straight to the club. It was still early so I laid on the couch in my office until the others arrived. I was falling asleep when Mikey and J-Money came in talking loudly. "Fuck. I almost got some rest."

"This isn't the time to be sleeping. We need to find out what we're going to do about Nina," said Mikey.

"I told you I'd handle it."

"Yea I remember but it's hard not to worry when my life is in your hands."

"I got us. What's up J-Money how's the tour life working out for you?"

"It's amazing bro. I am having the best time of my life. It's crazy people I've never even meant before show me mad love."

"That's credit to the work you've been putting in. Your fans appreciate it."

"No doubt."

"How long are you in town for?"

"As long as you need me to be?"

"What I need you to do is keep doing your thing. We'll handle things around here."

"Well if you need me call me. Were headed out to Vegas for a show tonight."

"Nice. Keep representing. I'm rooting for you."

"Thanks. I'll be in the main room while y'all handle your business." He shook our hands and said, "Later." When he exited the office, I turned my attention to Mikey.

"I need you to believe in me now more than ever. Do not give up on me now. I have a plan. I'll fill you in once it's set."

"I trust you bro. The situation is just getting to me. We aren't no gangsters."

"I know. It is getting to me too. After all we did our best to avoid a situation like this."

"Yea and that worked out for us great."

"I know things look hopeless now but that will change."

"I hope you're right."

I walked over to the coffee and said, "You want a cup?"

"No, I have to get out of here and run some errands."

"Okay. We'll talk later."

After he exited the office, I locked my door. I checked my safe to see how much money I had saved in the event I needed a Plan B. Plan B was to get as far away as possible. I had hoped it did not come to that but based on how things were looking it was better to be safe than sorry. I counted the money then put everything back in the safe and closed it. I sat down at the desk to continue thinking of what Plan A was. I needed help from someone who would dare go up against Nina. There was only one person I could think and that was Wendy Summer. I had found the number to the station and just needed the courage to call.

Before I could pick up the phone there was a knock at the door. I opened it and standing there was Natalie. She was stopping by before starting her shift. I told her, "Please come in." Before we could sit down, she was apologizing about what happened the other day with Casey. "You don't have to apologize for that asshole. You deserve better anyway."

"Thanks Pierce."

"I'm just glad I was here to help you."

"Me too." Then she kissed me.

That kiss reinforced that the other day was no fluke. We were on the same page. I kissed her back and we went at it on my couch. I stopped for a moment and got up and made sure the office door was locked because we were not going to be interrupted this time. I had waited for that moment a long time.

I stroked my hands across her silky skin as I kissed her on the neck. Then I helped her take off her shirt as she raised her arms overhead. I kissed down her torso slowly then gently took off her pants. Then I began squeezing and sucking on her succulent breast. She pulled my head up to her face and looked me in the eyes. "Lay down on the couch," she said. I took my shirt off and threw it on the floor. She started kissing on my chest down to my abdomen then my pelvic area. She unzipped my pants then pulled them off along with my boxers. She began to perform oral on me like I had never experienced before. However, I did not want to ejaculate

152

prematurely so I stopped her and said, "It's my turn."

I ripped her panties off, laid her on her back, and began my trip downtown. I could feel her body trembling as I did my best to please her. After the foreplay I put my manhood inside and was overtaken by her warm, wet, and enticing love. We went on for about ten minutes before I finished. Up until that point I do not think I had ever climaxed like that before. I did not know where it would go from there, but I did not want it to end.

My feelings for her had started to intensify. I didn't even want her working at the club anymore. I wanted her all to myself. I wanted to spoil her, but I understood it could not be. At least for now. Things had to stay the same. I had too much going on. On top of that I had a family that I loved more than anything despite how I was feeling.

After we finished, she left to get ready for work. I sat in the office and let that moment replay over and over in my mind. When I went into the main room J-Money was at the bar having a grand time like he always did. I hung out with him for a while talking shit. Just as Natalie hit the stage in came Casey. I hopped up and pulled him to the side to confront him.

"You have some nerve showing your face here after the other night." He got in because we had different guards that day who were unaware of that pest.

"I just came to apologize for the other night. I was drunk and made a huge mistake coming here and starting shit. I don't want you to think I'm some jerk off."

"You don't have to worry about that because I don't think about you at all. So why don't you take your bullshit apology and get out of here."

"Can I at least apologize to Natalie." I was outraged at the idea of letting him talk to her, but it was not my place to decide.

"You get one minute when she gets off stage. If you say anything to upset her. It won't end as nice for you as it did last time." I had security watch him until her set was over. When she came off the stage, I asked her if it was okay with it. I could tell from her face despite what he did she still felt bad for him. I could tell because that is the face I made for a long time for my mother.

We all went outside, and I gave Casey the floor to speak. "Nat, I want to apologize for my behavior toward you the other night. I feel horrible and understand if you never want to speak with me again. I am going to work on making myself a better person like you said. No more booze." He hesitated then said, "I can be the man you want." I loudly cleared my throat.

"Keep it to the apology. All that other stuff isn't necessary but anyway it sounds like we're done here."

"I guess so. Also, Pierce if you ever need any additional entertainment in the club, I am a music executive. I can make it happen for you." I gave him a head nod and we walked back inside with Natalie.

I pulled her to the side, and said, "You okay?" She placed her hand on my cheek.

"I'll be fine."

She went back to work, and I walked back to the bar. When I sat down, I received a text message from Ray that read, "I'll be back in town tomorrow evening."

"Okay. Meet me at CandyLand," I replied. After I sent the message, I turned my attention to J-Money. He asked, "So who was that guy you were talking to?"

"Old news."

"I take it, that's her old boyfriend."

"You could call it that." He looked at me with a smile.

"Chill bro he's gone. Is there something going on with you two I don't know about."

"It's nothing." I took a deep breath and signaled Natalie to meet me in the back."

When we were alone, she asked, "What's wrong?"

"Nothing. I rented a suite tonight downtown at the Lux Hotel. I was wondering if you wanted to spend the night with me." She smiled.

"I think I could do that."

"Cool. I'll be in room 404." I handed her the spare key.

"I'll see you in a bit."

I left the club and got in the truck then drove off. After I was out of the view of the club I pulled over to the side of the road. I called the station and asked for Wendy. They transferred me to her line. She picked up and said, "Wendy Summer. May I ask who's calling?"

"I have something you want to hear. Can you meet me at the Sun Diner in thirty minutes?"

"I don't even know who this is or what this is about?"

"I got info on Nina Williams. Trust me this is a story you do not want to miss. We can meet somewhere public. What do you have to lose?" She hesitated for a minute and said, "Okay. Can I at least get your name?"

"Call me P."

"Okay P. You better not be wasting my time."

"Don't worry I'm not. There is a diner in East Village called Café 24. Come alone and sit in the back booth. I'll see you in thirty minutes."

When I arrived, I parked across the street from the diner and waited for her to show up. Shortly after I saw her walk inside. I put my hood on, got out the truck, and followed behind her. When I got inside, she was sitting in the back booth. As I walked toward her the waitress asked, "Can I help you sir?" I pointed toward Wendy.

"I'm meeting a friend."

I sat down across from her and said, "Evening Miss Summer."

"I suppose you are P."

"I am."

I picked up the menu and asked, "What are you having?"

"Don't waste my time. I am not here for dinner. You said you had something to tell me. So, let us hear it."

"We're going to talk but you also have to eat tonight and so do I. Let us order something first?"

The waitress came over to our table and said, "How's it going tonight? What are you folks having?"

"I'll take a southwest chicken wrap with fries and a glass of iced tea." She looked at Wendy.

"And you?"

Wendy looked like she was starting to get annoyed, so I replied, "She'll have the same thing."

After she took the menus and left Wendy said, "I don't know what you're trying to pull but I came here for a story not a dinner date." She grabbed her things and began to get up.

"Okay. I'll start talking." The truth is I was stalling because I was not sure if I was doing the right thing. However, I had no other options.

She sat back down, and I said, "I know how she

transports her drugs in the country."

"Okay How?" I looked at her with a wary look on my face. "Look don't hold back now. You contacted me for a reason."

"The company is called Dash transport. The pickups usually take place twice a week on Tuesday and Thursday so they should be expecting a pickup tomorrow afternoon. The driver usually gets back around 3 pm. Shortly after her people will come in and make the pickup."

"What do you get out of telling me this?"

"Like yourself I just want her off the streets. I figured that you could use this information to make it happen and you would be the first one on the story. Sounds like a win-win to me."

"It appears that way. Is there anything else I should know?"

"No that's it."

"Okay. You better not be bullshitting me. If you can think of anything else, I believe you already know how to get a hold of me." The waitress came out with the food and Wendy got up.

"Enjoy your food."

She left and I sat there and ate alone. I had the extra meal boxed up for Natalie. I got in my truck and called the number on the cellphone Dame gave me. Surprisingly, Nina was the one who answered. I told her the meeting was set. At this point I had to wait for tomorrow to see what happened.

When I got to the hotel Natalie was not there yet. I put the food on the counter and took some time to relax before she arrived. I ordered a bottle of wine from room service and let it chill on ice. I also had rose petals from the doorway to the bed and chocolate covered strawberries in the fridge. As I sat on the couch with my feet up there was a knock at the door. I opened it and there she was. She had on a trench coat, and six-inch heels. She walked inside and said, "You didn't have to do all of this."

"Shhh. Special people should have special things. Just enjoy it." I offered her a seat on the couch and poured her a glass of wine. Then I started giving her a shoulder massage to help her relax.

After a few minutes I walked over to the fridge and grabbed the chocolate covered strawberries. I fed them to her and watched her lips wrap around it as she sucked and bit it. Next, I put one in my mouth and kissed her as she bit the other end. I took her coat off and underneath she had on sexy red lingerie. That was one of my fantasies. I thought to myself "Dreams do come true." I had her lay down on the couch and grabbed a piece of ice from the bucket. I traced the ice slowly all over her body followed by my tongue. I went from her mouth, to ear, down her neck, past her shoulder, to the breast, around the nipples, down her stomach, between her thighs and then I paused.

I started teasing her by kissing around her private area while avoiding contact. Her legs were wrapped around my neck while I was squeezing her ass. I could feel her body squirming and yearning for my touch. However, I was not ready to give her what she wanted yet. I put oil on my hands and began rubbing her gently. I could see the fluid dripping out of her.

Now it was time. I recalled her saying she liked to be fucked hard and I did not want to disappoint. I lifted her up and put her against the wall and began thrusting her forcefully. She moaned with satisfaction and I reveled in the sound of her voice while making my own sounds. Moments later I had her on all fours smacking her ass and holding her hands behind her back. I asked, "How do you like that?"

"A lot Daddy."

"You want me to slap it harder?" She moaned loudly.

"Yes!" I slapped one cheek and then the other. Watching that beautiful woman from behind was mind blowing. We finished in missionary where I continued to hold off until she couldn't take anymore.

We finished and laid on the floor appreciating the moment. We didn't even speak. We just stared at each other. I could not resist and had to ask, "How was it?" She looked at me with a blank expression then smiled.

"It was amazing. I loved every minute of it." That is all I needed to hear. That made my night. I felt like the man. If I did not think it would have ruined the mood. I might have gotten up and beat on my chest. To cap off the night we got more wine and hung out in the hot tub and talked through the night.

Chapter XIX

All Falls Down (Nina)

Today is the day I eliminate one of my biggest problems. Getting rid of Pierce and getting a new supplier will be one less thing for me to worry about. I rolled out the bed and grabbed my phone. While I was searching for Dame's number in my contacts an unfamiliar number popped up on the screen. I ignored it and they called right back. I was annoyed but now they had my attention. I answered the call and said, "Hello."

The automated message responded, "This is a collect call from the Los Angeles County Jail. Do you accept the charges?"

"Yea." Once the call was connected, I was silent.

"Things out of town just got complicated. I might be away for a while but don't worry I'm going to hold it down," said Jason.

"We'll make things right again. Keep your head up. I'll be in touch."

Then I hung up. Those calls are recorded so it was not a good idea to say too much on the phone. It was Jason calling to let me know that he was going to keep his mouth shut. I just hope for his sake it stays that way. One of my top guys was locked up and I knew they were gunning for me next. When he was arrested, I had my lawyer ready to wire his bail as soon as I found out.

However, it turned out he was not given bail because they felt he was a flight risk.

Despite my spot being raided and Jason being locked up. There was still business to be taken care of. I was not going to leave any money left on the table. I made some changes and sent some new people to run my LA territory. If there was ever a time for me to start thinking of an exit plan it was now. I found myself in a state of paranoia. For the first time I was uncomfortable in my own skin. I have become accustomed to being in complete control. However, I will not fold. I am made for this life. If anything, I will come out of this stronger.

Meanwhile, I remained in my Penthouse Suite until I figured out my next move. I poured a glass of cognac, sat down, took a sip, and leaned back on the couch looking out at the skyline view through my panoramic windows. Before I could get comfortable my phone started ringing. I answered it and said, "Mayor."

"Nina."

"You have any news for me about LA?"

"I've got nothing. It was not a local Pd operation. This was the feds and those guys aren't sharing any information."

"Damn. Well keep me posted if you hear anything."

"I will. I also recommend you lay low with everything going on because I'm sure they plan on coming for you next."

"I hear you."

"Okay, we'll talk soon."

After the call I decided to go to The Den and had Dame meet me there. When I arrived, I went straight into my office. When I walked in Dame was already there waiting. He passed me the blunt as I walked by him. I took two deep puffs and exhaled all the bullshit out. I passed it back and said, "It turns out that the bust was the feds not LAPD."

"Shit so what do you want to do?"

"There's nothing we can do about that. We just have to stay out the way. We will handle this meeting tonight and go from there."

"It's whatever. You know I'm with you either way."

"I know, and I appreciate that. Are our guys ready for tonight?"

"Yea I told them to meet us at the Den."

"Bet."

While we sat on the couch passing time, we smoked a couple more blunts. I started flicking through the channels until I saw the drug bust at Dash Transport. I looked at Dame. "Do you see this shit?"

"Yea. That's crazy."

"Today is when we usually make our pickup."

"Word. If they didn't have the product for our shipment that would have been us."

"For sure."

Now they are getting too close for comfort. Somebody must have it for me. After tonight it is time for me to start moving differently.

We walked out to the parking lot and our guys were waiting and ready to go. They were two young guys named James and Greg. We trailed behind them on the way to the meeting at an abandoned warehouse in Mira Mesa where I used to do deals at. It was isolated and low key just how I liked it. During the ride Dame asked, "We're doing the right thing right?"

"It is just another day of business. We have done this plenty of times before. Just focus on the job in front of us."

"Word. You are right. Just another day in the office."

"Yes sir. Don't start going soft on me."

"Never that. Besides how could I ever be soft around you." I looked over at him and we laughed.

"Whatever that's supposed to mean." We lit another blunt and played music for the remainder of the ride.

As we were approaching the building, I did not see any other cars parked. My guys parked first, and we pulled up right beside them. Before we got out, I sent James and Greg in to make sure it was a go. Me and Dame watched as they entered the building. Moments later they signaled us to come in. I looked over at Dame and gave him a head nod. We got out of the car and entered the warehouse. In the middle of the room was Pierce, an Asian man, and a big guy I suppose was his muscle.

"Hey Nina. How are you tonight?"

"I'm not here for the small talk. How did you get here with no car?"

"We were lost and ended up parking on the other side of the building. Trying to find the entrance. It's dark so you probably passed us on your way in and didn't notice."

"Maybe. Is this Ray?"

"I am. Nice to meet you. Pierce tells me you're in the pharmaceutical business and are looking for a supplier?"

"I am."

"Are you currently renovating this building for the business?" Confused by what he meant I looked at him sideways. That is when Pierce chimed in.

"That's not important Ray. Let's just stick to the business."

"Right. Sorry. What drugs are you looking for?"

"Maxy."

"Okay. My company deals exclusively with opioids so that would not be a problem. What is the name of your company?"

"What do you mean?"

"If our businesses are going to work together, we'd need to know what pharmaceutical company we're contracted to." I looked at Pierce as he stood there uneasy looking away from me.

"I'm the company. I do not know what you heard but I run these streets. I can make you way more money than Pierce." Ray looked confused as if he were caught off guard.

"I see. Can you give me a second while I talk to Pierce?"

"Is there a problem?"

"Not at all. I just need to go over a few things with him."

I let them have their chat and from the look of it Ray was displeased. Dame whispered in my ear, "Something's off."

"Yea I feel it too but they're not your usual dealers so let's see what happens." I waited cautiously as they conversed. After some time, I looked at my watch and noticed it had been a couple minutes. "Do we have a deal or what?"

"It's all good. There was just a little mix up that is all. Right Ray?"

"Yea. Sorry about that." Then he walked over to me and said, "How much will you need?"

"Let us start with three hundred thousand pills a month for now and go from there. Can you make that happen?" He looked at Pierce then turned his attention back to me.

"I can."

"So, it's a deal?" He gave me a faint smile then extended his hand out.

"It's a deal." I reciprocated the gesture and we shook hands.

"Don't worry Ray, our business won't present any risk for you. I have friends in high places in this city. You'll be protected." Pierce then presented me with a bag

"And to welcome our partner in good faith. Here are fifty thousand pills," said Pierce.

"You're just going to give me fifty thousand pills?"

"Give no. It is part of the three hundred thousand you requested. You can pay for it all when you get the other two hundred and fifty. I know you're good for it." I asked dame to grab the bag. Then I directed my focus back to Pierce.

"Keep that phone I gave you close by and I'll tell you were our next exchange will be."

As Dame was driving us out the industrial park he said, "So what do you think of the new connect?"

"I don't know. He's different than what I'm used to but maybe it'll be easier than dealing with the Cartel."

"Yea I hope so. What do you want to do now?"

"Go back to my place and keep laying low until all this stuff blows over." When we exited the industrial park, we were swarmed by police vehicles and officers yelling.

"Put your fucking hands up now!" All I could think

about was the bag of pills in James and Greg's car. They may finally have something on us. They stood outside of both our cars demanding us to exit the vehicle slowly.

When I got out with my hands up. One of the officers grabbed and threw me on the ground.

"You don't have to be that rough. I was getting down."

"Shut up Nina. If you want to be a man. I'll treat you like one." I was already restrained and not resisting but he still used excessive force while putting on the handcuffs. My face cringed but I did not say anything else. I was not going to be baited by him. He was hoping I kept running my mouth, so he had a reason to rough me up. I do not understand how this could happen. It was just another day. Another job. What changed. From there all sorts of ideas ran through my mind. Could it be somebody in my organization, was its McDonald or Wallace, did Pierce set me up, or could they just have outsmarted us. Anything was possible. After he lifted me up, I saw that the badges had San Diego PD on them. This was a local bust not federal. I knew for sure this was not a coincidence. Somebody set me up. How else would they know I would be here?

We were all taken away in separate cars. On the way to the station I could not help but think about if this would be the last time, I was free. When I arrived at the station, I was brought straight to the interrogation room. They had me sit there for a while before coming in. I guess they thought that would shake me up, but I was not saying shit. I know how this goes. I was not falling for it. I just had to stay calm and patient. I would be out of here soon. I just hoped that James and Greg did the same.

When the detectives came in the room, I knew they had nothing on me. There were two of them. It was your typical good cop bad cop routine. Detective Miller was the hard ass and Detective Smith was the charming one. Smith was pretty sexy though. In different circumstances she may be one of my girls. Miller on the other hand came in being brash. He clearly did not respect me but that was fine. I did not like his ass either. If he was not a cop. I would fuck him up.

The first thing he said was, "It's all over. We got your dike ass. So, you can keep playing the tough guy or save yourself."

They kept asking me to confess to having intent to distribute the pills found in the other car. They insisted I ran a major drug organization and was in cahoots with the cartel. However, I stuck to my story. My response was, "I don't know what you're talking about. That wasn't mine and I don't know them."

I wanted to know a little more about what they thought they knew so I engaged with them a bit. "What is it you think you have on me?"

"Let's stop fucking around. We know you have expanded your business all throughout California that is why you're here and soon or a later we will put it all together. It's just a matter of time," exclaimed Miller. Then he added, "Don't be foolish. Your guys are probably giving you up right now. Give us something and we can help you." They had the right idea but nothing to prove it. They were working hard to put me against Dame and the others, but I knew that when it came to Dame, he was going to hold it down. He would never flip on me for some bullshit promise from them. Our bond is deeper than that. When we got into this

167

game, we knew what it was. I am my brother's keeper and he is mine. As far as James and Greg they knew what happened to rats.

"Why throw your life away protecting everyone else when we're going to take you all down anyway. You have a chance to save my time and yourself now. This offer won't be on the table forever," said Miller.

"What are you offering me?"

"Give us the men who supply you and some other major players from other organizations that you work with and we can offer you a deal." I smiled.

"I told you already. I don't know what you're talking about." They were offering me a deal that could possibly result in immunity based on what I told them, but I was not going for it. I knew they had nothing and would eventually have to let me go.

"Look I know you think you're doing the right thing but really you're making it worse for yourself," said Detective Smith. She was almost convincing but not quite. I stared at her and made sexual innuendos while she talked.

"I like it when you talk dirty to me, detective." Miller slammed his hand on the desk and grabbed me by my collar.

"Enough with the bullshit. These are serious charges you're facing. No one else can save you but us."

"I appreciate your concern, but I'll pass. I want to speak with my lawyer."

"Let her go, Detective Miller. She's not worth it," said Smith. He let me go and threw his hands in the air.

"We can do it the hard way." As I sat there in silence, I watched as he paced back and forth around the room.

"You really think you're a tough guy. When we are done with you, you are going to wish you would have picked up a Barbie instead of hanging out with the fellas. Bro."

I wanted to punch him in his face, but I did not let it get to me. It was not the first time somebody repeatedly made those types of remarks toward me. At the end of the day he was mad because they had nothing. I stared back at him with an arrogant smirk on my face until he stormed out. "I hope you understand what you're doing," said Smith.

"Hey. When I get out of here how about we go out for a date." She shook her head side to side with an exaggerated grin.

On her way out of the room I said, "You didn't say no though. I'll be in touch." Truth is I did not know what I was getting myself into. I did not know what they actually had on me or where my future went from here, but I chose this life and when I leave it will be on my terms.

Eventually, they moved me to a jail cell. I didn't even get a chance to make my one call. The officer pushed me in the cell. The sound of the steel doors slamming shut symbolized what I have dreaded since I got in the game. He had me position myself with my back toward the door so he could remove the cuffs. Before walking away, he said, "Get comfortable. You'll be here for a while." I started rubbing my irritated wrist after spending hours in those cuffs. When I looked up there was another girl in the cell already.

"First time in," she said.

"You could say that."

"My name is Rachel. Nice to meet you."

169

"Nina."

"What are you in for Nina?"

"Being at the wrong place at the wrong time." She laughed. I laid back on the hard bench looking up at the bottom of the top bunk.

"I guess that's why we're all here," she replied. I was standoffish. I did not come to jail to make any friends. This was just a small detour. She did not seem to mean any harm but talking to much is what keeps you in jail. "You from the city?"

"Yea, sure."

" Look I'm just making conversation. I do not have an agenda. Time passes slowly when you're just sitting here alone."

"It's nothing personal. I am just not in a good mood. There's other places I'd rather be."

"Understood." I sat there wondering what my next move would be.

The next morning a guard came to the door. "Miss Williams you made bail and are free to go." I got up and did the necessary paperwork for my release. When I walked out those gates I did not look back. There was a yellow taxi waiting for me. When I got in, I asked the driver, "Who sent the car?"

"I don't know his name. I was told to tell you a friend." I thought to myself that whoever this friend is it is clear that my freedom is in their best interest. The driver pulled over on a side street and stopped. "This is your destination."

"Where? There is nothing here."

"I was told to bring you here and he'd take over from there." I was uneasy getting out of the car but what the heck there was nothing easy about this situation.

I stood on the street for all of a minute when a black SUV pulled up. I got in and there was Mayor Wallace and Police Chief McDonald. "I need to get Dame out."

"We're already working on it. You are in the clear for now. It looks like the other two guys who were found with drugs in their car aren't going to talk but we may need a more definite solution," said Mayor Wallace.

"I'll handle it."

"The funny thing is you keep saying that and look at our situation now," said McDonald.

"You can't blame all this shit on me. It is part of the business. It is the risk we all take. Plus, it was your department that busted me. Where was the heads up?"

"I wasn't informed of the bust. Apparently, the tip came at the last minute and they acted without my authority. If you would have laid low like we said. This doesn't happen."

"Like I said I'll figure it out."

"You better because I don't take risks. I eliminate them."

"Is that a threat?!"

"That's a promise." That is when Wallace chimed in.

"Look, neither one of you is helping our situation. We need to deal with the issues at hand. What's your plan to get things back on track?" I sat there silent for a moment while pondering ideas.

"Did Pierce get busted at the industrial park too?"

"No why?"

"Because now I'm pretty sure he was the one who had me set up. Maybe he has bigger balls than I gave him credit for."

"Really Pierce again?"

"Who else knew about Dash transport and my

171

meeting with him at the industrial park. Besides us and him?"

"True."

"He has to go before he takes us all down with him."

"Okay we'll handle it, but you gotta lay low. This situation is getting too hot and uncomfortable for all of us. Can you do that?"

"I got you."

They dropped me off a block away from my apartment. While walking into my penthouse, I received a call from Dame. It felt good to hear his voice. I said, "Are you good?"

"Damn you can't say hi first." It was good to see he still had his sense of humor.

"Hey Dame. You good are what?"

"Never better."

"I bet. Hang tight. I will have you out and back soon. I'm working on it now."

"Cool. I heard you got out and wanted to check in."

"Yea some friends came through."

"Word. Be Safe. I'll see you soon."

"Later."

I entered my penthouse and one of my guys was waiting for me in the lobby. I had him come upstairs while I grabbed the money out the room to be delivered to my lawyer for Dames bail. I could not let Dame sit in there while Wallace worked on it at his own pace. After a restless night in jail I was exhausted. I fell asleep on the couch and woke up to a call from my lawyer. He updated me on the status of Dame's bail. He would be getting out first thing tomorrow morning and when he did our people would be there waiting to get him back.

Now I was awake and sitting in the penthouse alone. It was starting to drive me crazy. Laying low was not for me and I needed to be around good vibes. My people needed to see me, so they know I am still running shit. I could not afford to appear weak now. That would make me vulnerable. I called one of my finest women Coco. She was perfect for this occasion. When she answered I said, "Get ready? We are stepping out tonight. I'll be by to pick you up in an hour." I got fresh like I always and went down to the garage. I hopped in one of my exotic sports cars. I went by Cocos place and when I pulled up, she was ready to ride. She was flawless. Gorgeous face with a tight body and had on a sexy red dress to compliment it. When we got to the club this time I walked in through the front. I wanted to make an impression. When we walked up the red carpet, I was all smiles and flair. I greeted a few special guests and walked to my section.

As me and Coco sat there enjoying ourselves. One of my guys came over to me and said, "Nina. There's a guy out here demanding to talk to you."

"Does he look familiar?"

"Nah, I haven't ever seen him before."

"You get his name."

"Jose."

"Bring him around the back into my office and pat him down."

I told Coco, "Keep having fun. I'll be right back."

When I walked into the office Jose was seated in the chair. I walked in, sat on the corner of the desk and took my time before I said anything. I had to check him out first. I do not like new faces. Especially new faces I have never seen.

"What can I do for you Jose?"

"Miguel sent me."

"For what?"

"Well for starters you're making us look bad by seeking out other suppliers as if we can't take care of our own. Then the Dash transport bust. We were under the impression you ran this city so how could this have happened if you didn't want it too?"

"Since I can tell you know a lot about me. Then I am sure you know that my organization has been taking major heat as well and I just got out of jail. So yes, I agree there is a problem, but it isn't me."

"What do you think this problem is then?"

"Do you know a man named Pierce who used to work for Dash?"

"The driver?"

"Yes, but he's so much more than that. It turns out he has his own operation and is our biggest competitor."

"Maybe that's why he didn't show up for the pickup that day. There was another driver. He must have known the bust was coming. What else can you tell me about him?"

"He has a strip club called CandyLand. That's where I would start."

"Okay. I will tell Miguel about our conversation. We're done here for now."

"No problem. Thanks for coming by." There was a lot going on and I was not sure where I stood in this equation. I went back out to my section and told Coco, "Let's dip."

When we got back to my spot I said, "You can stay with me tonight." I could use the company and did not want to be alone. She smiled.

"I'd love to."

"Good. There's that beautiful smile." She nudged me on the arm.

"You're so stupid. I must be beautiful all the time because I'm always smiling."

"Not at the club. You were in there mean mugging." We laughed.

"That's because I was waiting for you."

"Oh, that's what that was."

"Yup."

When we got inside the penthouse she wanted to shower. I grabbed her a towel, wash cloth, and something out of my closet to wear. I cooked us broccoli, chicken, and rice. When she came out of the room, I already had the table set. "You were in there for a while."

"The water felt good. I didn't want to get out, but the food was smelling so good."

"You're full shit." We laughed.

"You like how I did that."

"Yea alright."

She looked down at the food and said, "Look at you. You out did yourself."

"That's why I started a restaurant in the first place. I do this."

"I'll be the judge of that but thanks again for tonight Nina. I needed to get out."

"The night is not over yet. How does it taste?"

She took a bite and said, "It's delicious. Anymore because I'm going to need seconds."

"Yea it's more on the stove. We can eat that after we work up an appetite again."

"Mm. Desert sounds better than dinner."

"You don't have to wonder about what you can find out right now."

"You are too full to put anything else in your mouth." I dropped my fork, grabbed her hand, and led her into the bedroom.

I took her shirt off exposing her soft perky breast and began kissing on her neck. I kissed slowly as I held her waist. I continued as I listened to her breaths get deeper and more rapid. Then I pushed her onto the bed. Following that I tossed my shirt and pants on the floor. Before I joined her, I pulled her pants off and gently laid on top of her with my breast gliding against hers as I kissed her luscious soft lips. I put my leg between hers and our thighs rubbed as she thrust her hips into me. I could feel her nipples stiffen up as I worked my way down twirling my tongue around them.

I tenderly bit her nipples as I sucked them while rubbing my fingers across her soaking wet private parts. I continued to work my way down while squeezing the inside of her thighs. I put my head between her legs and said, "I think I'm ready to eat again." I dove in and began twirling my tongue on her. She thrusted her private parts against my face and was met with the same force. She moaned and screamed loudly with extreme pleasure, "You're the best." I watched as she had climax on top of climax until her knees buckled and could not take it anymore. When I finished, she laughed and said, "Come here."

I laid next to her and said, "Now I'm full."

Chapter XX

After School (Pierce)

Luckily, last night worked out well. I took a huge risk not telling Ray that we were going to meet with a drug dealer. Nonetheless, she is locked up now and my family is out of harm's way. Wendy Summer had come through for me in a major way. Now I had to hope that the pills I gave her would stick. I was in uncharted waters and hoped that I could withstand the tide.

On another note the last couple of days I had spent with Natalie were amazing. It was night and day from my relationship with Riley. I felt like when I was with her, I could be myself completely. She respected me and did not make me feel obligated to change. She listened, gave compliments, and went out her way to oblige me. The thing I liked most about her was unlike Riley who was constantly busy. She was always available. Having her in my life was eye opening.

However, a part of me felt guilty about allowing myself to develop feelings for her despite being married. To my defense it was not planned. It just happened and I am glad it did. In the midst of everything going on I wanted to do something special for her that day to show my appreciation. I called Natalie and said, "Hey Big head. Do you have plans today?"

"Other than waiting to see you. I just have to run a

few errands. Why what's up?"

"I want to do something for you today."

"And what's that?"

"It's a surprise."

"Sounds good to me. I can be at the hotel around five o'clock. Is that cool?"

"That's perfect." I wanted that evening to be a time she would never forget.

My first stop was to get a gift from the jewelry store downtown called Luxe. They say diamonds are a woman's best friend, so I got her 18k gold necklace with ninety diamonds in it totaling to two carats. It set me back like twenty-five thousand dollars, but she was worth it. Afterwards I had Terry meet me at a café nearby. I wanted to hear his opinion on our relationship. He had been through a similar situation and I felt like he had some insight I could use.

While I sat in the café awaiting his arrival. I noticed I was developing a heightened sensitivity to seeing couples. With everyone that passed me I felt more guilty about my newfound happiness. Society has a way of convincing you to sacrifice your own wellbeing to conform to the "norm." Whatever that meant. I constantly had to remind myself about what I learned in therapy. My reality and feelings are the norm. What is abnormal is going against it and accepting ideals that are not my own if only to fit in. When Terry walked in, I yelled, "Right here."

He walked to the table and said, "Long time no talk. How are you?" I got up from my seat and embraced him.

"I'm Okay. You?"

"I'm actually doing pretty good. How's the family?"

"Everyone's good thanks. Yours?"

"Honestly. It has been great since the baby. I'm a lucky man."

"Good. I'm glad to hear that."

"So, why'd you call me down here?"

"I have a dilemma and I thought you'd be the right guy to talk too."

"What's the dilemma?"

"It's about a woman."

"I assume this woman isn't Riley."

"Well at least I know you're paying attention." We laughed.

"Before you say anything. My advice is not to do it."

"I didn't even tell you the story yet."

"You don't have too. Experience has shown me it is a waste of time. You will never be satisfied. You always will need more. Just to find out you already had what you were looking all along right in front of you." I felt like he may be right, but it did not matter. I was already falling for her. I took the liberty of showing him the gift I got her.

"Wow. You are not fucking around. I'm curious to meet this woman now." I laughed.

"I can't get her off my mind."

"Clearly."

"You never felt like that with any of the women you stepped out on Carol with?"

"No, they were just a fling for me but the one time I let myself be infatuated with another woman. I made a fool of myself."

"Why do you say that?"

"Let's just say I was chasing a fantasy that wasn't real."

"I hear you, but this isn't a fantasy, it's a dream come true."

"As long as you're thinking with your head on your shoulders and not your dick then maybe you should see where it takes you. How'd you afford that thing anyway?"

"Things have changed a lot since the last time we've had a chance to hangout. I have not had a chance to thank you. Thanks in part to your referrals. Business has taken off. You risked a lot doing that for me."

"Truthfully, you did me a favor. It turns out I was being investigated but by the time they started to pursue me I'd gotten rid of most of the patients just looking for a fix." Then he paused for a moment and said, "I hadn't noticed how long it's been since the last time we hung out. These past couple of years have been a lot for me with work, the baby, and my marriage. Time has just sort of been passing me by. I say all that to say. Sorry I've been a shitty friend."

"Stop. It is understandable we are men with families and responsibilities. We're not college kids anymore."

"I guess you're right. Anyways I need to get back to work. Hopefully, we all can get together soon. It was great seeing you." We got up from our seats and said our farewells.

When I got myself together, I headed over to the hotel. I watched a comedy show on the tv to try and ease my mind. In the beginning of the second episode Natalie walked in. She had on a tight black skirt and a white blouse that showed just the right amount of cleavage. I was so happy to see her. She gave me a passionate hug and I asked, "What did I do to deserve this greeting?"

"I'm just happy to see you."

"I'm happy to see you too. By the way you look beautiful. I love the outfit." She smiled.

"Good because I got it just for you."

"I have something for you too." I walked over to the couch, grabbed the box, and handed it to her.

"What is this?!" She opened it and screamed. "Is this real?!"

"Yes, it's real." She jumped into my arms, hugged, and held me tight.

"I don't know what I did to deserve this but thank you so much."

"I'm glad you like it. Let me help you put it on?" She gave me the necklace and turned her back to me. I placed it around her neck, and she turned back around. "Wow. It looks amazing on you."

"Take a picture so I can see." I pulled out my phone and took a picture. She looked at it and said, "This is cute. Send it to me so I can post it on my social media." I laughed then texted her the picture.

"So, what do you have planned for us?"

"I thought we'd go to Black's beach."

"Let's do it."

"Have you ever been?"

"No but I'm familiar with it."

"You're about to get really familiar with it today."

"Why are smiling so hard?"

"Because I can't wait to see you with your clothes off." She playfully slapped me on my arm.

"Shut up."

"Do you want to grab something to eat first?"

"Yes, I'm starving!"

"Cool. I got a spot for us to go."

When we walked out to the parking lot she asked,

"Where's your truck?"

"It's parked in my garage. I decided to switch it up." I pointed at a shiny black classic muscle car that I had finished rebuilding a year ago but never drove because Riley could not stand how loud it was.

"What do you think?"

"It's awesome. When did you get this?"

"For about two years. I've been waiting on a special occasion to bring it out."

She kissed me and exclaimed, "Well what are we waiting for. Let's go!"

We went to a nice Italian restaurant by the beach that was so delicious. I enjoyed every minute of the food and conversation. While looking at her I could see a future I knew we could never have. My heart struggled with my mind to live in the moment. When we got to the beach I parked on the street. Then I rolled the windows up and put on the ac. When I pulled a rolled up blunt out of the dashboard she said, "We can't do that here?"

"Relax nobody cares plus it'll be legal soon."

"Keyword. Soon." I lit it anyway, took two puffs, and passed it to her. She hesitated then took a puff and started coughing. I began laughing hysterically while patting her on the back and offering my soft drink. We sat there passing it back and forth for about five minutes and then I finished it on my own. By the time we got out of the car I felt like I was floating. We took our shirts off, walked down to the sand, and started chasing each other around having a blast. What made it even funnier was looking at the expressions of all the other beach goers. They probably thought we were crazy.

Eventually, we calmed down and walked barefooted on the beach where the water meets the sand.

182

We talked about everything that came to mind. We were on the beach for hours. We sat down in a secluded spot and I said, "How was your day?"

"This was great Pierce. Today has exceeded all my expectations. It was an almost perfect day."

"Why do you say almost? Something wrong?"

"Not necessarily. I just wish I could spend it all with you."

"Well I'm yours now." She pushed me down in the sand and got on top of me. Then she whispered in my ear, "It's my turn to take control."

"Wait. Can anyone see us?"

"Nope." I tried to lean up and kiss her, but she stopped me. "Relax." She pushed me back down and I laid there as she stood up. She started teasing me by dancing in front of me seductively. Then got back down on top of me rubbing her fingers all over my bare chest while kissing on my abdomen. I tried to place my hands on her, but she pinned them both down with hers. As she continued kissing me, I began to get restless with anticipation of what was to come.

She pulled off my shorts and began rubbing on my private area. She looked at me and smiled. "Somebody missed me," she said.

I was rock hard and ready to go. She sat on top of me and slid me inside of her. It was instant euphoria. She rode me while I squeezed her ass. We went at it for about five minutes and when I told her I was about to cum she didn't stop until I got it all out of me. My face cringed as I emptied. When we were done, we laid back on the sand and gazed at the sky.

Our day together ended when my phone alarm went off reminding me it was time to pick up Junior from the afterschool program. I dropped Natalie off on the way at her apartment in Five Points. I was early so I sat on the side of the car for a few minutes until he was dismissed. When school was dismissed, he ran to me. I lifted him in the air and hugged him. I noticed his shoe was untied so I took a moment to tie it. While I was tying it, I heard tires skidding in the background. When I turned around and looked. I saw two masked gunmen with guns hanging out of the window.

Seconds later I heard multiple shots go off. I dove on the ground covering Junior. As the shots rang it was like everything was standing still. When it finally stopped. Junior said, "Daddy am I okay." I looked at him immediately in panic. When I looked down, I could see the blood on his shirt. I lifted his shirt and saw he was hit in the chest. I pulled out my phone speaking frantically to the 911 operator. By the time I hung up he had stopped breathing. I started yelling while performing CPR, "Someone help! I need a doctor!" I was in disbelief. I refused to believe he was gone. I held him tightly, rocking back and forth until the paramedics arrived. I told him, "You'll be okay buddy." I knew I was to blame for this. It was the first time I had blood on my hands, and it was my own. Things would never be the same.

Chapter XXI

My Baby (Riley)

When I arrived back to the states, I was exhausted. I turned my phone on and it was flooded with messages. I needed a minute to prepare for the mayhem I called life. I turned the ringer off until I got home. I could not wait to see my baby. It was nine o'clock in the morning on a Saturday. I came home to an empty and abnormally quiet place. I figured Pierce must have been out with Junior. I went into the kitchen and poured myself a glass of water. I cannot explain the feeling, but something just did not seem right.

I knew something was wrong. I put the glass down and picked up my phone. I called Pierce and got no answer. I looked at my text messages and saw a message from a friend that read, "Is Junior okay? I heard about the shooting at his school." I was confused and had no idea what was going on. I was in the complete dark. I ran to the TV and turned on the news. The report was about a child who was gunned down yesterday at Juniors school.

There was no further information released about the victim but deep down inside I knew it was my baby. However, I did not want to believe it. Pierce still was not answering his phone and I did not know what to do. I tried not to panic by telling myself, "It isn't him." After all there was no official word that it was my son. I sat on the floor staring at the wall for about ten minutes when I heard the door unlock and open. I got up and looked at Pierce as he walked in with his head down and shirt covered in blood. His arm was in a sling and there was a bandage on his left shoulder. "Where's Junior?!" His eyes began to get glossy.

"He's gone." I started crying.

"What do you mean gone. Gone where?"

"He's gone."

I knew what that meant. It was confirmed. He was the boy who got shot. I blacked out and before I knew it, I was screaming, destroying everything in the house, and punching Pierce. He stood there and took it. When I was finished, I walked slowly to the couch in a daze. It felt like the walls were caving in on me and the world was ending.

"How did this happen? What did you do?" He stood there in silence with tears pouring down his face. "You need to tell me something."

He struggled to speak but in a hoarse voice he replied, "I don't know."

"I think you do."

"What is that supposed to mean?"

"You know exactly what it means. This is not some random shooting. You were the only two shot. It must've been targeted." He exploded with anger.

"What do you mean! You think I wanted this shit to happen and it is all my fault! You do not get to do that! I lost my son today too!"

"Well you didn't do anything to prevent this." I could see the guilt on his face there was something he was not telling me.

"He's at the funeral home in Hillcrest." I did not have anything else to say to him. The mere sight of him disgusted me. I grabbed my bag and left the condo.

I went to see Junior at Hillcrest. When I arrived, I received a call from Ray.

"Hey, I heard about your Junior. I'm sorry and give my deepest condolences."

"Thanks."

"How are you feeling?"

"Like I let my baby down. I wasn't there for him Ray and it hurts."

"It's not your fault. Have you had a chance to speak with Pierce?"

"Yes."

"Did he say anything?"

"No. He's acting like it's some random shooting."

"Okay. I need to talk with you whenever you're up to it."

"About what?"

"It's too much to get into over the phone but it's something you need to hear."

"Okay. We can meet after I leave the funeral home."

After hanging up I cleared my throat, wiped my tears, and tried to pull myself together. The walk to the door seemed like it was a mile away. When I entered the mortician said, "Hello Mrs. Kennedy."

"How do you know who I am?"

"Your husband called and told me to expect you. I am sorry for your loss. I have him downstairs all cleaned up if you want to see him." I just nodded my head in agreement.

He led me down the hall into the basement. I was terrified to enter the room but when I did, I saw him lying peacefully on the table. I immediately broke down into tears. I hoped that he did not experience any pain. I touched his body softly and dragged my finger across his face. I said, "My little angel." I had flashbacks of his smile and laughter. I missed him so much. I hated myself for all the time I did not spend with him and hoped I was a good mother. I cried as I held his little hand in mine. I sat there for as long as I could staring at him until the mortician said, "I'm sorry Mrs. Kennedy. I know you're experiencing tremendous pain and though I sympathize with you for your loss. I must close up in preparation for tomorrow."

"Of course, I understand. When do you open in the morning?"

"At eight."

"Okay. I'll be back here first thing."

When I got back into the car I started sobbing. My hands started to tremble, and I began to experience a state of paralysis. I thought about him being helplessly shot and me not being there for him. I questioned if I deserved to be his mom, how could Pierce let this happen to our boy, and how I could move forward from this. I was swamped with a barrage of thoughts which made it impossible to think. I began to be so overwhelmed I started slamming my hand on the steering wheel and yelled out, "Why!"

I needed a distraction. Something to get my mind away from the torment. Even if only for a moment. I called Ray. "Let's meet now."

"Where are you at?"

"I'm on the side of the road on Fourth Avenue a block away from the funeral home."

"Okay. Stay put I'll be right there." I sat there

waiting for him trying to keep it all together.

After fifteen minutes I saw lights from a car approaching me from the rear. Ray got out and entered my car on the passenger side. When he got inside, he said, "Hey Riley. How are you doing sis?"

"Not good but I guess that's expected right."

"Yes, it is. If there's anything I can do for you don't hesitate to ask."

"I appreciate that Ray. What is it you said you wanted to talk about?"

"It's about Pierce," he said tentatively.

"What about Pierce?"

"I don't think any of this has happened by coincidence."

"What does that mean?" He momentarily looked away and took a deep breath. "Don't hold back now. Tell me what you know."

"He was in trouble, so he set up a meeting with him, me, and a drug dealer named Nina. He told me that she threatened to kill him and his family so he set her up and this might be a retaliation."

"Why didn't you tell me this before?"

"I didn't think it would lead to this."

"Well it did, and not only did it get my son killed but now I have to worry about me getting killed. On top of that you put our family and the business at risk by getting involved with a drug dealer." I paused for a moment then said, "Get out the car Ray. I can't stand to look at you right now."

Before he got out of the car he said, "I understand you are heartbroken and angry but don't do anything crazy like go after this woman Nina. She made a remark about having friends in high places in the city so be careful."

When he got out, I was overtaken with anger and grief. I was not going to let his death go unpunished. I am still his mother and he will get justice. I thought deeply about who could help me. I grabbed my phone and called a law school friend, Deputy Attorney General of California Manny Suarez. The phone rang seven times before he answered and said, "Hello. This is Deputy Attorney General Manny Suarez. Who am I speaking with?"

"Hey Manny, it's Riley Kennedy."

"Hey Riley. I am sorry to hear about your loss. How are you doing?"

"Truth be told. Not good."

"I couldn't imagine. I will keep you and your family in my prayers. How can I help you?"

"I came across some information that could help solve the case of my sons shooting."

"Did you already call the local police department?"

"No, I haven't."

"Well that's probably where you should start."

"The thing is they may have something to do with it."

"What do you mean by that?"

"I was told a drug dealer by the name of Nina might have been behind this and that she is protected by some powerful people in the city so I felt it would be better if I asked you to look into it directly."

"Why would she want to kill your son? And who is your source?" I could not tell him it was my brother, but I had to make it convincing, so he would take me seriously.

"I don't know why my son was killed but the

person who told me said that they were a part of her organization. I guess they had a guilty conscience."

"Okay. I will see what I can find. Give me a couple days and don't repeat this to anybody."

"Thanks Manny. I really appreciate this."

"Don't mention it. We'll talk soon." I hung up that phone with a new purpose. For now, on its family first.

Chapter XXII

Way Out (Pierce)

A chilling feeling of disappointment has taken over my body. I was extremely tired but could not sleep. The horror of losing my son is not something I could have ever imagined. I stood on the balcony looking at the view I adored for years but now being on it left me in agony. The thought of jumping off to get rid of the pain weighed heavily on me. The silence of the condo bred sadness in my heart. No more sounds of Juniors laughter as he played around our home. The only sounds now were the cries of me and his mom.

I am riddled with madness and guilt that is almost impossible to bear. There lies an emptiness in me now I may never be able to fill. I wanted a way out but first my son needs justice. I looked down at my phone blown up with messages. I disregarded them all and called Mikey. I let him know I needed to meet ASAP at CandyLand. Before I left, I asked Riley, "Do you need anything while I'm out?" She ignored me as she sat on the chair in our bedroom staring out the window. For the first time she was right about me. I would understand if she never talked to me again.

I pulled in the back of the club and received a call from Dr. Shaw. I directed her to voicemail. I did not feel like it was a time for words. I needed to act. When I got inside the club Mikey and our team came up to me and gave their condolences. I said, "As you all can see things have just got serious. The very thing we tried to avoid is here so if anybody wants to leave now, I understand." You could hear a pin drop in the room after that comment. I looked around the room in the eyes of all my men and watched as they all stayed down with me. I continued to say, "I appreciate you all for standing with me but if you're as sorry for me as you all say. You'll help me find out who did this."

I walked away into my office and left them there to discuss it amongst themselves. I knew this had something to do with Nina and my attempt to set her up. I wanted to strike back. However, even though I was emotionally detached from reality I still was not crazy. There was no way I could kill her without risking the life of me and everyone I cared about. While I sat at my desk Natalie barged into my office.

"Are you okay? I have been trying to call you all day. I'm sorry to hear about your son." Then she hugged me, but I did not reciprocate the gesture. She stepped back and looked at me. She could see that the Pierce she knew was gone.

"Thanks, but I need a little space right now." She looked at me with a worried stare.

"I know that look. What are you thinking about doing?

"I'm just mourning my way."

"It won't bring him back. Nor will it take the pain away. If anything, it'll make it worse."

"What do you know? You haven't experienced this type of pain before?"

"You're right but I've seen what losing my brother

to gun violence did to my father. He forgot about everyone else that cared about him. Now he is in jail. What good is that?"

"Well I won't be letting anybody down. He was all I had, and he was taken from me."

"Pierce. This may be the wrong time to spring this on you, but I love you. I care about you and I do not want to see you hurt. There are other ways to deal with this." At the time I showed no emotion and continued on as if I did not care. I was not ready to hear that. I needed to stay focused for Junior.

"What do you expect me to say to that?"

"I just thought you should know."

"Well I don't feel the same. There is no future for us. You're a stripper for goodness sakes." When I said that she looked as if someone had just taken the life out of her.

"Given the circumstances I won't take your disrespect personally, but you need to reevaluate this situation and think about what Junior would want." She walked out and I sat there in silence looking down at my phone. It was not right but I was treating her that way because I wanted her to leave. Her presence was clouding my judgement.

Moments later Mikey came in after her. "You good bro?" I looked at him with a blank expression on my face.

"How can I be good if the people who murdered my son are getting away with it?"

"That's not what I meant. I saw Natalie run out of here and I wasn't sure what had happened."

"You don't need to worry about that. Do you have any new info on who did this to me?"

"We're working on it. Our guys are out there putting their lives on the line to figure it out."

"They need to work harder then."

"I know you don't want to hear this but we're still running a business here that we built and at the moment it's falling apart."

"I don't give a fuck about the business right now."

"I know you want pay back but retaliating with violence isn't us. We are normal guys who sell drugs. We're not built for this street shit."

"Speak for yourself. Nobody is making you stay Mikey. I can handle this on my own." He did not respond and stared at me with a scowl on his face.

What he was saying made sense but at the time it was just noise to me. I agreed with him, but I had other plans in my head. I left the club and went back to my condo to check on Riley. I did not bother calling because I knew she would not answer. I stopped at the grocery store on the way to get some of the things she liked with the hope that she would eat something. I could not stop thinking about the pain my actions have caused her.

When I got home, Riley was gone. There was a stench in the air from the trash that had not been taken out for days. I tied the bag and put it by the door. When I walked in the bedroom, I noticed that her luggage bag and some of her things were gone. I assumed she could not deal with the constant memories of Junior. She was gone.

I could not process how my big dreams had turned into a nightmare. I do not know how things got so fucked up, but it did not make sense to make it worse. I knew nothing good could come from this. I needed to get away for a little and figure some things out. It was time to go back to CandyLand to get my stash. I got in my truck and drove there. I went into my office and grabbed my gun and the half a million dollars I had in the safe. That is when I heard yelling in the main room. Shortly after Mikey came running in the office and said, "It's the police." I did not know what to say or do. Karma is a bitch. They say things happen in threes. First, I lost my son, then my wife, and now I was about to lose my freedom.

I stood there having a borderline anxiety attack when Mikey grabbed me and said, "Let's go!" We went out the side office door onto the back-patio enclosure and over the wall before they got to the office. We got into Mikey's car and did not look back. When we were in the clear he yelled, "Woooo! Fuck that was close. We just got away."

"Yea for now. The clubs in my name. After they find all the pills in there I am done. I need to find a way out of the city ASAP."

"What about Nina?"

"I'm not sure but I'll figure it out. Just watch yourself out here. Stay safe." We said our goodbyes and he dropped me off at Natalie's apartment.

Luckily, she was not at the club during the raid. I banged on her door and when she opened it, I rushed in. "What's wrong," she asked? I told her about the raid, and she was in disbelief.

"What did you do?!

"Nothing out of the ordinary."

"What are you going to do?"

"I don't know but I need to figure it out quickly."

I went into the bathroom and splashed some water in my face. I stood at the sink looking at myself in the mirror. I did not recognize my reflection. I did not know who I was anymore. I was so far gone I did not know if I ever would again. Moments later she knocked on the door. "Is everything okay in there?"

"Yea just give me a minute." I felt like a rat in a maze. I could not think of a way out."

I laid low in Natalie's apartment before making a move. Meanwhile I called Riley. Even though we were not on good terms. I had to let her know about the pills that were more than likely confiscated in the club. After a brief conversation she asked me to meet her at Tony's Pizzeria to talk.

Later that evening when I walked in the restaurant, she was right there. I was happy to see her, but I wished it were under different circumstances. She had two slices of cheese pizza, one for me and one for her. I sat down and watched her put parmesan cheese on hers. She loved it. She is the one who introduced it to Junior. She looked up at me and I said, "How are you?"

"As good as I can be Pierce."

"I'm sorry Riley."

"I know."

"No. I haven't been completely honest with you or myself." At that moment I took responsibility for destroying my family simply because I could not cope with my reality and see how blessed I really was. I was worse than my parents. I had it all and gave it up because I wanted to be seen as a success. I continued on to say, "I did this to us, and I can never make it right. It would have never happened if I..." She interrupted me mid-sentence.

"No, we did this Pierce. The onus is not just on you. We can go back and forth about all the things we could have done better, but I would rather not. Let us just try to move forward. Let us focus on honoring our child and getting justice." We smiled at each other with tears in our eyes.

"When's the funeral?"

"Tomorrow."

"I wish I could be there with you, but my presence would only ruin it."

"I'm aware of your situation."

"I'm sorry I didn't mean to get you caught up in this."

"Don't worry about me. I can handle it. What are you going to do?"

"I have no idea. I figured I would go back out east but they were looking for me everywhere. I can't get out of the city." She placed her hands-on top of minds on the table.

"I can help you with that. You can use the company jet while the service is taking place, they won't ever suspect it but after that you'll be on your own."

"Thank you."

"It's what Junior would want."

Before seeing her, I did not ever think we would be able to speak again. I knew then that through us his memory will always live on. As our conversation came to an end I said, "I miss you Riley. A lot."

"We have been together a long time and it wasn't always bad. We had shared a lot of good moments. You'll always have a place in my heart Pierce." The way she looked at me I knew I did not want to hear what she was about to say. She continued saying, "We need to move on and if I'm ever going to have any chance at a happy life again. We need to make our separation final."

Then she handed me papers. "These are divorce papers. I need you to sign them."

I did not give her any pushback. I hate to admit it but at this point I was only dead weight for her. I grabbed a pen and signed the papers. "Were we good parents?"

"I like to think so. We wanted the best for him. I just hope he knew how much we loved him."

"He knew I made sure of it. I may have given you a hard time, but I always let him know mommy is not here because she is providing for our household. Then I'd tell him that if she could she'd spend all of her time with you because she loves you so much." I took a napkin and wiped the tears off her face."

"Thank you Pierce I needed to hear that."

"By the way you were an amazing wife too. I was just to blind to see it."

"You weren't so bad yourself." I finished the conversation by saying, "Just know you have a friend in me and if you should ever need me, I'm here for you."

She hugged me and said, "Take care of yourself Pierce." We held each other long and tight. I did not want to let her go but now it was too late.

Chapter XXIII

Man Down (Nina)

Dame getting out has been the only good thing that has happened for me in a while. Unfortunately, Jason was still locked up and since being arrested things had gotten too hot. It was to the point I could not even re-up. No suppliers wanted to deal with me until they felt I had my operation under control. As a result of this the streets were starting to dry up. Customers were starting to become uneasy. Some even started seeking a new dealer. Despite my empire crumbling before my eyes I had bigger problems. I was now the number one target on the feds radar, and I needed to figure out a way to get off of it. It was to the point that Police Chief McDonald and Mayor Wallace could not even help me. I had to find another way.

While me and Dame sat there watching the news. It was no surprise that Wendy Summer made us the highlight of the show. However, what got my attention was the details of our operation that she knew. The police did not even know Dash was how I was smuggling my drugs in, so she definitely had an inside source and I had an idea who it was. It had to be Pierce. I called one my guys and instructed him to get me a location on him. Meanwhile I was going to pay Miss Wendy Summer a visit.

After about an hour of waiting outside of the station she finally came out. I got out of my car, put on my shades, and followed her. I kept my distance as she got on the trolley. I stood on the opposite side of the cart while trying to keep an eye on her amongst all the people. She got off on the second stop at fifth avenue. I followed her a couple blocks to an impressive loft building. When she scanned into the building, I grabbed the door as she extended it open. When she turned around to look at me, I looked away in the other direction as if I thought someone else was coming in behind me.

When she got to her door. I anxiously awaited as she sorted through her keys looking for the right one. I creeped toward her as she turned her key inside the lock and pushed her inside when the door was opened. She immediately yelled, "What are you? What do you want?" I raised my gun and pointed it at her.

"Lower your voice." Then I took off my shades. "You know exactly who I am. You spend enough time talking about me."

"Not by choice. What do you want?"

"Who's your source?" She acted as if she had no idea of what I was talking about.

"Source for what?"

"The source who told you about my operation. It's funny how you were the first one on the story and quickly linked the bust to me." She turned her head to the side and sighed.

"Can you at least put the gun down so we can talk like civilized human beings?" I smirked at her and lowered my gun. She offered me a seat on the couch and sat on the chair across from me. We awkwardly looked at each other for a moment before she said, "I don't know the guy's name. He told me he used to work for you and had information on your organization."

"What did he look like?"

"I don't know it was a phone tip."

"What did he sound like?"

"I don't know. Like a normal guy."

It was clear she was not going to say his name, so I threatened to take her life. That is when she told me about the Deputy Attorney General personally going around looking for information on me and my accomplices in the drug world. She was not going to admit to knowing Pierce, but this information was equally important, so I thanked her for her time. When I got back to the car my phone started ringing and it was Naja. I ignored it and shortly after I received voicemail. I listened to it and understood her level of concern for me, but I needed to keep my distance. I could not bring anybody I loved into my drama.

When I got back to the Penthouse Dame was still there laying low. Before greeting me, he said, "Bad news. The governor was on TV talking about his dedication to putting an end to the war on drugs. I'm afraid that we might be the example he's trying to set."

"Nah. He's always talking that same shit. It's politics."

"That's what I thought at first too. Until I just got a call from our people at the Den. The feds were in both of your places of business looking for us."

"No fucking way. They don't even have shit on us."

"I don't know but we need to figure out some shit like right now. What is up with the Mayor and Police Chief. What the fuck are we paying them for."

"They think were hot and keep saying their hands are tied"

"Fuck that. They need to do something. After all, if we go down so do, they." He had a point and we needed help. It appeared that they were the only option. I called them to set up a meeting and they insisted we met at an abandoned warehouse on the outskirts of the city.

When me and Dame arrived, we saw two cars there already, so I grabbed the bag and we walked in. They were both standing there awaiting our arrival with uneasy facial expressions. I approached them and said, "Gentleman thanks for meeting us."

"What's in the bag," asked McDonald?

"It's your payment."

"For what. We have already been paid for this month."

"Look at it as me showing my appreciation for our partnership."

I handed over the bag to Mayor Wallace. "We have a major problem. We need to figure what we're going to do about it."

"We have a problem. No, you have a problem," said McDonald.

"Must I remind you we're in this together. Last time that I checked you're just as involved in this as me. Also, it turns out that the Deputy Attorney General is asking around about me and my accomplices in the city."

"And how do you know this," asked Mayor Wallace.

"Wendy Summer told me."

"Well you better do something about it because you fucked up and were not going down with you," exclaimed McDonald.

"Watch your tone," said Dame.

"Fuck you. And if I don't," replied McDonald.

"Let us all just calm down and figure this out. There is enough blame to go around but Nina McDonald is right this is not our problem. You're the one who insisted on expanding to LA and going after your competition."

"I made that move in the best interest of our business and I didn't hear you two complaining when the money was coming in."

"No, you made that move based on pride and greed. Now after a reality check you come to us demanding our help," Wallace replied. Then he threw the bag of money down by my feet. "Were done with you. It stops here. You're a bigger problem than your worth."

In the corner of my eye I saw Dame move his hand to his side and that's when McDonald reacted by shooting him at point blank range in the head. It all happened so fast the next thing I knew I was in the car speeding off with no destination. I was in complete shock. I could not believe what had just happened. I wanted to retaliate but I was not able to. I could not even go back to get his body. I was finished and I knew it. I was out of the game and had nobody. Luckily, I grabbed the bag which had a hundred thousand dollars in it before running off. Leaving me with enough money to get lost. I needed to get as far away as possible.

As I was leaving the warehouse, I came to a fork in the road that had an arrow pointing left to San Diego and right toward Phoenix. My best shot was to turn right and not look back. However, if I ran now, I would be running for the rest of my life. I could not let Mayor Wallace and Police Chief McDonald get away with this. Our business together was far from over.

Chapter XXIV

Back East (Pierce)

My time in San Diego had come to an end. I no longer had a reason to stay there. During the flight I thought of everything I was leaving behind Junior, Riley, Natalie, Terry, Rich, Mikey, J-Money, Dr. Shaw, and CandyLand. I had built and destroyed my life in San Diego. Now I am going back East for the first time in years attempting to rebuild it. I planned on staying in Philly since I knew they would be looking for me in AC. Thanks to Riley I made it there in one piece.

When I arrived, Zoe was there to give me a ride. After days of hiding out and worrying it was nice to see a familiar face that represented good times in my life. Just like when I was a child, the sight of her gave me comfort. I was staying in Kensington. Zoe set up an apartment for me there to stay. I really hated bringing her into this situation, but I did not have anyone else. She was all I had.

On the way there we reminisced about old times. She knew how to keep my mind at ease. That is why I love her till this day. When I saw the place, I was staying I jokingly said, "I know I want to lay low but not this low." She laughed.

"You can always stay outside." I looked out the window at all the trash, worn down infrastructure, drug addicts, and homelessness that plagued the community. Though I have never dealt drugs here I felt guilty for my contribution to the problem. I sat there quietly with a blank facial expression. "I was just kidding."

I turned my attention to her and replied, "I know."

"About your situation I did some digging and they're planning to charge you for possession with intent to distribute a controlled substance."

"Is that so."

"This is serious. You are looking at some real time in prison here."

"I know. Don't worry. I'll figure it out."

"I hope so. Also, there is one more thing you should know." She waited until the end of the ride to tell me so I knew it would not be good. "It's about Betty." I immediately cut her off.

"Look I have enough problems. I cannot deal with her right now. Tell me about it later."

"That's the thing. I'm telling you now because there might not be a later."

"Is it another overdose?"

"No actually she's been clean for some time now but she's not doing well. She had nowhere to stay so she's been staying with my parents." Lost for words I did not respond and remained silent. She went on to say, "She didn't want me telling you about this. Believe it or not she's actually sorry."

"Please, you believe that?"

"Well, I let you know. Do with that information as you like." I must admit I felt bad for her, but I could not risk making myself more vulnerable by taking on another problem.

I thanked Zoe for the ride, got the apartment keys,

my two bags, and got out the car. The building I was
staying in was a brick row home. The neighboring house
was boarded up and abandoned. I thought to myself, "I
may be actually worse off now than when I was a boy in
AC living in section 8 housing." It was a shit hole, but I
wanted to lay low and I could not get any lower than
this. I walked inside, dropped my bags and walked
down to the corner store. As I walked, I thought of
Junior. I had visions of him running and playing.
Because of those memories I could still smile in my
worst moments.

Before getting to the store there was an overpass. I
stopped and looked out below. From the overpass I
could see multiple drug addicts standing around
slumped over. It looked like a zombie apocalypse. In my
peripheral I saw a man laid out on the sidewalk who did
not look good. I actually thought he was dead. I walked
down to see if he was okay. As I approached him there
was a horrific stench. It smelt like feces, urine, vomit,
and garbage all in one. While holding my nose I grabbed
a stick and poked him for a response. I said, "Hey. Are
you okay?" Initially he did not answer.

Then I poked a little harder and he popped and
yelled with a raspy tone, "What the fuck is your problem
man. Can't you see I'm sleeping."

"I'm sorry." I turned around and when I looked
under the overpass there was a drug encampment.
There were quite a few people, worn furniture, trash,
and too many used needles to count.

On the way back up to the overpass I looked in the
hollow helpless eyes of a woman sitting in a tent with
her legs curled up and wearing filthy clothes. I thought
of my mom and imagined how she struggled with

addiction. I sympathized with her. While I stared at her and we made eye contact. She asked, "Are you holding?"

I gave her money and said, "Here's enough to get some food, new clothes, and a room for a couple nights to clean yourself up." I knew she would likely just blow it all on drugs, but I had to try and help. I walked from beneath that overpass enlightened. These people are not bad. They are sick. Holding a grudge with my mother would not benefit me at all. It is best I confront it and for once tell her how I feel. I owed it to myself. If what Zoe said was true, I needed to act before I ran out of time.

When I got to the store. I grabbed some food and hygiene products to get me through the next couple of days. While walking down the aisle I saw a kid who reminded me of myself. He was wearing oversized dingy clothes and was stuffing candy in his hoodie. I walked up to him and in a low tone I said, "Take that stuff out of your pocket." He froze and before he could run, I grabbed his arm. At the bottom of the aisle was the store employee who I signaled to stop. I said to the boy, "Don't be scared I'm not trying to get you in trouble. I am going to let you get whatever you want. Just bring it to the register." He came to the counter with packs of candy and chips. "You sure that's all you want?" He did not respond and looked at me with uncertainty. "Today is your lucky day. Don't hold back now." He went back in the aisle to grab cakes, and drinks. After paying I said to the store employee, "Thanks."

When we got outside before giving the kid the bag I said, "What's your name?"

"Billy."

"Well, Billy. You almost got yourself in trouble back there."

"So, it wouldn't be the first time," he replied arrogantly.

"What are you stealing candy?" He stood there in silence, mean mugging me. "You want the bag, right?"

"I don't have anything to eat at home."

"Where's your parents?"

"I don't know."

"Who do you live with?"

"My grandmother."

"You can't get food from her."

"She doesn't have any money."

"Okay." I gave him the bag and asked, "Do you want to earn some money?"

"Woah mister I'm not into that."

"Into what?"

"Selling my body." I laughed.

"I would hope not. I just want you to look out for me. If you see any strange cars or people out here let me know."

"Like cops."

"Yea like cops."

"How much are you paying?"

"How about ten dollars a day?"

"Twenty and we have a deal."

"Deal." I extended my hand out and we shook on it. I gave him forty dollars and said, "Here's a two-day advance. I'll meet you here around this time each day." As he walked off, I said, "And stay out of trouble."

When I got in the apartment I looked around. Zoe had already furnished it, so it made up for the outdated interior and appliances. Ultimately, I was lucky to have a place to stay so I could not complain. I took my duffle bag with the money and hid it in the freezer. I sat on the couch and looked in my other bag to see if I had any weed, but I was all out. The only thing I had was a sack of pills. I turned on the tv and that is when I got the craziest idea in my life.

I decided to take two of them to see what all the fuss was about. In about ten minutes I began to experience euphoria like never before. It numbed my pain and made everything seem calm. It felt like I was floating in paradise. For a moment everything was fine, and I dozed off. I woke up a couple hours later and started vomiting. I had trouble breathing and tried to calm myself down. I stumbled into the bathroom and splashed some water in my face. Then I sat down against the wall and focused on my breathing.

After some time, I was able to get back up. I grabbed the pills and flushed them all down the toilet. That would be the last and only time I would be using them. Now that I was situated, I called Natalie to make sure she got the money I left for her. I left half of my money which was nothing compared to what she deserved. The phone rang a couple times before she answered. I knew we were not on the best of terms before I left San Diego, but her happiness and well-being was important to me. She picked up but didn't say anything, so I said, "Hey. How is it going?"

"It's going."

"Did you get the bag I left you in the bedroom."

"Yes, I did. Thanks."

"What have you been up to?"

She replied with an annoyed tone, "Why did you call me Pierce?"

"Listen. I am sorry for how things were before I left. I was an asshole to you, and you deserve better

"That's an understatement."

"I'm glad we had a chance to be a part of each other's life. I wish I could do more for you." She was silent for a moment. "Are you still there?"

"Pierce there's something I have to tell you."

"What is it?"

"I don't know how to tell you this but I'm pregnant."

"Are you sure?"

"Yes, I'm sure."

"Is it mine?"

"Are you serious? You're the only person I've been with."

"I didn't mean anything by it."

"Of course, you didn't."

"I'm sorry. It caught me off guard. Are you going to keep it?"

"Absolutely. Is that okay with you?"

"I just thought that because of our situation it would be best not too."

"It's not our situation, it's yours. I gave you up already. I refuse to give up our child. Whether you're here or not."

"You both would be better off without me anyway. I don't deserve a family." She sighed deeply.

"Hey. I have to go. Call me when you stop feeling bad for yourself."

She hung up leaving me on the line with the dial tone and I said, "Bye."

For me to have any hope of moving forward I needed to deal with my past. I took the Rail-line from the 30th St. station to AC. The ride was about an hour and a half. When I got to AC it was not quite like I remembered. It was not as busy with tourists, some of the casinos were closed down, and there were more homeless people. I got off the train and caught the bus to Zoe's parents' house. When I got nearby, I stood across the street for a moment. The house was light blue with a big white front porch that was aligned with flowers I helped plant, and next to it was a driveway we used to play in. As I looked at the house I was flooded with memories. I hated the fact that I was returning on these terms. I did not know what to say to them. I know they expected more from me.

On top of that I felt like I let Betty down too. The fact that she was the farthest thing from a mom to me did not matter. It turned out that the apple did not fall too far from the tree. When I approached the door, Michael opened it. I could not tell from his face, but I knew he was disappointed. "Welcome home." When I walked inside standing there was Agatha. She walked over to me and gave me a hug.

"It's so good to see you. Can I take your bag?"

"No, it's okay I'll hold it. It's good to see you both but I wish it were on better terms." I knew they had already known why I was back in town. I was embarrassed and ashamed. As I stood there with my head down, she placed her hand on my shoulder.

"We're sorry for the loss of Junior. Are you doing okay?"

"I'm doing my best to cope with it."

"If we can help in any way let us know."

"I know. Thanks."

"Well your mother has been waiting for you. She is

upstairs in the guest room you used to stay in."

"Okay and thanks again for everything you both have done for me and my mom."

"Don't mention it. Your family to us and we look out for our own." I smiled back at her and walked up stairs to see my mom.

I was nervous and did not know what to expect. I entered the room and there she was helplessly laying in the bed. I walked over to her and placed my hand on top of hers. She slowly turned her head toward me with a faint smile. At this point she was weak and frail. "Hey Betty. How are you?"

"Hey Pierce. I am okay. How are you son," she asked in a soft tone.

"I'm hanging in there. What is wrong? Nobody's telling me anything."

"I'm just a little under the weather." By looking at her I knew it was much more than that. The feelings I had were reminiscent of those I felt watching dad toward the end of his life. I felt sorry for her. I knew she was not all she could have been for me, but I hated to see her suffer. When I looked away to collect myself, she said, "Don't feel bad for me Pierce. I put myself in this position." As a tear rolled down Bettys eye she said, "You're my greatest accomplishment. I'm sorry I didn't ever show you that." My heart dropped. I waited forever for her to embrace me.

Despite this I knew her praise was empty. As for it have not been for her illness, she probably would not have said anything. Nonetheless I still respected her effort to restore what chance of a relationship we had left. "Some accomplishment I am."

"Why would you say that. You have far exceeded

anything me or your father could have imagined."

"Your expectations must've been pretty low." She started coughing.

"Is something bothering you son?"

"It's nothing."

"Whatever it is, it can't be worse than the things I've done. I'm sure you can fix it."

"Maybe." When I looked over in the doorway Michael was standing there.

"Pierce, I need you to come downstairs."

"I'll be right down." I turned my attention back to Betty.

"I have to go now."

"Before you go can't you call me mom one time like you used to when you were little." I hesitated for a moment.

"Okay Mom. I'll be by to see you again." Then I kissed her on the forehead.

On my way out. I took the bag of money and put it in the bedroom closet. When I got downstairs Michael said, "It would be better if we go on the porch." When I exited the house, I was met by Zoe's husband. I did not imagine our first-time meeting in person would be this way. He read me my rights and placed me under arrest.

As we walked to the car, Agatha said, "We're sorry it had to be this way. We had no choice."

"You did this to yourself son," added Michael. I did not blame them though. He was right. I did do this to myself. I made my bed and now it was time to lay in it. My last sight of the house I pretty much grew up in was Betty standing in the window with her hand on the glass. I was back to the bottom where I started.

Chapter XXV

Closure (Riley)

Life without Junior has not got any easier. However, I do not suspect it ever will. There are some moments of peace but far more of pain. I deal with it day to day and try my best to live with it. Still there has not been any arrest or suspects named in his murder. It's time I take the matter into my own hands. With help from a friend who works for the San Diego Superior Courts I was able to get Nina's address. She lived in a Penthouse in the Marina District. I decided to pay her a visit despite how dangerous it was to pursue her on my own.

When I arrived outside of her home, I looked into my bag to check if I had my gun, I had recently purchased it for my protection. I walked into the lobby of the building and was approached by the attendant. "May I help you?"

"Yes. I need to get up to the Penthouse. Can you show me where to go?"

"Who are you looking to see?"

"Nina."

"Is she expecting you?"

"Yes, she is."

"Okay. Follow me over to the desk so I can check and see if she left a message for us to do so." I stopped him as he began walking toward the desk.

"Look. I am her lawyer and she is really pressed for time. She's going to be upset if she finds out I'm late because of the attendant downstairs."

"I am following our protocol for visitors. It will only take a moment." That is when I reached in my bag and extended my hand out with a hundred-dollar bill in it.

"Can you just take my word for it this time." He hesitated and looked around the room before taking it.

"Okay just this one time. Right this way." He led me to the elevator that went to the Penthouse.

As the elevator started to climb to the 32nd floor I grew more anxious. When the doors opened, I was surprised to find myself already in her suite. Before stepping out I looked around and saw no one. It appeared as if she had not been home in some time. It was a longshot, but I walked around looking for something that could possibly be proof that she murdered my son.

While I was searching in her living room, I heard something coming from the room. I stood still for a moment and the noise stopped. I reached in my bag and grabbed my gun and walked slowly toward the door. The door was slightly cracked open, so I pushed it with the tip of my gun. I entered the room and on the other side of it was Nina standing there with a gun pointed at me. "Why are you here," she asked?

"I just want to talk."

"About what? Riley."

"You know who I am?"

"Yea. You are Pierce's wife. Where is he?"

"How do you know him?"

"Let us just say we worked together."

"What do you want with him?"

"We have unfinished business.

"Would that business have anything to do with the killing of my son?"

"What are you talking about?"

"Don't play dumb. You tried to kill Pierce and ended up killing my son in the act."

"I don't know who told you that but that wasn't me. I would never kill an innocent kid."

"I know it was you. You're the only one who has a reason to try and kill him."

"If you think that's the case then you truly don't know your husband."

"Are you implying there are others?"

"You catch on fast."

"Who did it?"

"I'm not sure exactly. I can think of a couple people who may want him dead but that's not any of my business I have my own shit to deal with."

"Is that why you're hiding in your own place?" She stared at me and did not respond. "If you help me. I will help you." She lowered her gun and then I lowered mine.

She hesitated then replied, "I may be able to help."

"Okay. What do you want in exchange for this information?"

"I want you to negotiate immunity for all my crimes."

"How do you expect me to do that?"

"You'll see when I show you who did it."

She walked over to her closet and went into a safe. She handed me an envelope. I opened it and inside were pictures of the Mayor and Police Chief receiving payments from here and email documents linking them to transportation of drugs at Dash.

"This tells me nothing about my son?" She pointed at the bottom of the page to an email from Mayor Wallace that read, "Don't worry about Pierce we'll take care of him." I was in disbelief, but I held myself together.

"I'll need a copy of this, but they will more than likely want your testimony."

"I understand that."

"Okay. I'll let you know when the deal is set."

As I was leaving the penthouse she said, "I truly am sorry about your son."

When I got in my car, I called Deputy Attorney General Manny Suarez. "Hey Riley. Is everything okay?"

"I found out who murdered my son."

"Who was it?"

"It was the Mayor and Police Chief."

"Those are some strong acquisitions. Where did you hear this?"

"From Nina."

"That's your source. I thought you said she murdered your son?"

"I was wrong it wasn't her."

"You can't possibly be trusting the word of a drug dealer."

"She gave me proof and agreed to testify."

"What does she want in return for this?"

"A deal where she doesn't serve any time."

"This case will not exonerate her from her charges."

"She also has solid evidence that they were the ones transporting the drugs into the country."

"If that is the case, we may have something to talk about."

"I have one more favor to ask. This Police Chief was the same corrupt cop who claimed to have found the pills at my ex-husband's bar. He should be released pending further investigation."

"I will definitely look into it for you. I want you to come straight to my office right now so we can finish this conversation."

"Okay. I will be there shortly. Thanks Manny." I hung up the phone feeling a bit of relief. This does not change what has happened to Junior, but it is a step in the direction for justice.

Chapter XXVI

Set Me Free (Pierce)

I was sent back to San Diego and held in jail for about a month. It gave me the opportunity to really get to know myself. I spent most of my time reading, writing, and thinking. I could not stand being trapped in a little cell with another man and no privacy. I could not even shit in peace. In addition, the food was horrible. To make matters worse the culture was just like the streets. There were drug dealers and addicts in here too. On the brighter side it seemed like I was in the clear of any retaliation from my enemy. I had heard about Nina being run off. It was a matter of time before she got what was coming to her.

Now I needed to find a way-out jail. I kept hope even though I knew it was unlikely with the representation my public defender was providing. He was a nice guy, but it was clear he was overwhelmed with the amount of cases he had, so I did not expect much from him.

While I was sitting in the cell reading a book about introspection the guard dropped off my mail. I grabbed the letter and noticed it was sent by Mikey. I had not heard from him in a while and was happy to have some mail on Christmas eve. I opened the letter and when I got to the middle of it, I was hit hard with devastating news. He was informing me that J-Money was gunned down in his own neighborhood during a robbery. I would like to say I was shocked, but I was not. I always told him he had to move on from his old life now that he was somebody. He did not understand everybody is not going to be happy for your success. He insisted nobody would touch him there. I wish he were right. I dropped the letter and dropped my head into my hands. For me it was reminiscent of my son. I did not do enough to save him.

I sat there still until it was time for my first substance abuse group therapy session. I found myself in group therapy because of a failed drug test when I got locked up. They found marijuana and opioids in my system. This session was just like the other ones from the previous two weeks until I passed out.

I woke up in the infirmary. When I opened my eyes, I noticed I was hooked up to fluids. I asked the nurse, "What happened?"

"You passed out during group therapy."

"How?"

"The doctor believes it's from dehydration and lack of nutrition." I was terrified. I never passed out before. I thought it was the end. "How are you feeling now?"

"Better now. Thank you." When I looked up, I saw the Deputy Attorney General talking about an investigation of corruption in the San Diego Police Department and the city's politicians on the news. It turns out they were being linked to the drug problem in San Diego. There was no mention of Nina. Shortly after the guard came over to me.

"Your lawyer is here to speak with you." I figured he was just here to sell me on taking the plea. I still was not willing to accept twenty years though.

When I was able to get up, they took me to the consultation room. While entering the room I said, "No deals." When I got inside, I saw he was with another man this time. This guy was clean shaven, wore a black suit, and had a serious look on his face.

I sat down and my lawyer said, "Hey Pierce. This is Agent Gonzales from the DEA. You may want to hear his deal."

"I'm listening."

"I could use your help Pierce," said Agent Gonzales.

"Help with what?"

"With taking down the Cartel. We can protect you."

"I don't know anything about them, so I guess I don't need any protection."

"We both know that's not true. They know about you giving information about their organization that led to the bust at Dash. You really think they're going to let that go?" Up until that point I had no idea that they were aware of that.

"I don't know what you're talking about."

"You know exactly what I'm talking about. You can sit in here and wait for your past to catch up with you or help yourself. This is the best deal you are going to get. This offer will not stand past today. How long do you think you will be safe in here? And what about your family?" He had a point. I did not want to gamble on the idea that he was bluffing. I also certainly could not let anyone else get hurt because of me. He had my attention now and I was ready to hear him out.

"He's right Pierce. This is your best deal. If we go to trial it will not end well with the evidence, they have against you," added my lawyer.

"If I was going to consider it. What does this deal consist of?"

"You will have to share everything you know about Dash and be a witness. Eventually you will have to take the stand. If you come through on your part of the deal you will get immunity." I sat there for a moment and weighed my options. It seemed like I was screwed either way but at least this deal gave me a chance at some sort of life.

"I hear what you're saying but I need to see it in writing."

"Absolutely. Your attorney has the paperwork. You just have to sign." He passed me the paperwork and a pen. I skimmed through the document and everything looked good. Ironically, these papers were supposed to set me free, but I felt like I was signing my life away. I signed it and pushed the paperwork back across the table. Agent Gonzales reviewed it then looked at me. "It looks like we're all done here. I'll see you shortly."

When he exited the room my lawyer said, "You're going to be transferred today. Good luck." The guard took me out the room to prepare for my release. I did some more paperwork then was taken out of the building to where Agent Gonzales was awaiting to relocate me. He led me to his unmarked vehicle and loaded me in the back. I found it odd that the driver did not say anything or look back at all. I figured he was just another uptight fed. As we were exiting the gate I turned around and could see a guard chasing after our vehicle trying to flag us down. I told the agents, but they ignored me. We rode a few miles away from the jail and he pulled off the road into an empty lot. There was no one else around us and I knew something was wrong.

While looking straight ahead Agent Gonzales said, "You've caused my boss a lot of trouble. The set up at Dash and stealing business from him was not smart. You should have known better."

"Who are you?"

The driver took off his glasses and turned around pointing his gun at my face. To my surprise it was Jose. He shouted angrily, "No hay vuelta atrás hijo de puta!" Just as I thought I may have something to live for again I am reminded of my certain fate. However, I am not surprised because deep down inside I knew it would come to the point when my misfortune would catch up to me. This time I could not run from it. For the first time I embraced it. Just like those I envied the most it took dire circumstances for me to truly see what I have done. I looked down the barrel of the gun and watched as he cocked it. "Say hi to your son for me." BOOM! I was finally free.

Acknowledgements

After two and half years I was finally able to complete my first book. When I began writing this book, I wanted to do something for myself and on my own that I could be proud of. This accomplishment is a milestone in my life, but I found out that this is bigger than me. Though I was the one putting in endless time and effort to write it. It is the love, support, and encouragement I received from those around me that carried me through the process. If you take anything from this story, I hope that you see that we do not have to take on the burden of life alone. There will be times we doubt ourselves and feel discouraged, but we must not lose our faith. Last but not least thank you to all the readers who took the time to read my story. Stay tuned there will be more to come.